The Ghost Miner's Key

Angeli Perrow

To Kyle & Ayla –
Decode the mystery!
Angeli Perrow
2014

ISBN-13:9781480248410
ISBN-10:148024841X

DEDICATION

For Noah, my charming and imaginative
grandson

ACKNOWLEDGEMENTS

Many thanks to the Werly family, owners of the Techatticup Mine in Nevada, for keeping history alive, and especially to Shauna for the grand tour.

Chapter 1. The Haunted Mine

A coyote howled in the distance, an eerie, mournful sound.

Mandy crowded a little closer to her cousin Nick who was leading the way down a sandy path to the old mine. The sun had already sunk behind the rocky hillside and the blue shadows of dusk crept across the desert.

"I never realized how creepy it is out here when it's getting dark," Nick said, his eyes darting from one mysterious shape to another. "The cactus kind of look like zombies coming to get us." He gave a nervous laugh and jangled the keys. "I'm glad Dad trusted me to lock up the mine. He said he'd check it later when he gets back from Nelson, but meanwhile he didn't want any after-hour tourists snooping around. The company could get sued if someone got hurt in there."

"So, Nick," said Mandy, "this is the *ghost* mine you told me about? Are there really ghosts?"

"Well, I haven't seen any yet, but I've only been in the mine a few times. If violent death is what makes a ghost, this place should be full of them. When this mine was active, Forgotten Gulch was so lawless, no sheriff in Nevada would come near it. There were fights and shootings every day!"

He stopped in front of a rusty steel scissor gate. Beyond it gaped the dark entrance of the mine like a giant's open mouth. Nick pulled the metal gates together with a clang and turned the key in the lock. "Now we have to go to another gate around the hill," he said. "There has to be a second way out in case of a cave in."

"Nice thought," said Mandy, shivering in the deepening gloom. The ghost town was quiet – too quiet. With the tourists gone for the day and Uncle Ross and his boss away, she and Nick were the only two people there. . . at least the only two still alive. Another shiver tiptoed down her spine.

The coyote howled again.

"That sounds closer, Nick," Mandy said, grabbing the back of his sweatshirt. "Do coyotes eat humans? Or is it a wolf?"

He stopped and she bumped into him. "I don't think coyotes eat humans. . . unless they're desperate," he said. "But it might not be a coyote *or* a wolf."

"What is it then?" Mandy asked in alarm.

He shifted from foot to foot. "It might be a dog from h-e-double hockey sticks."

"Huh?"

"Well the story goes that the miners had dogs and they didn't treat them very well. They were chained up to protect the miners' possessions and claims. When the miners moved away, they abandoned their dogs. Some of the dogs were left in chains and starved to death." He gulped. "They supposedly came back as ghosts to get their revenge – the H-e-l-l Dogs of Eldorado."

As they approached the back gate, a low growl came from behind a rock a few yards away.

"Uh, oh," said Mandy.

"Come on!" yelled Nick, racing down the path to the gate.

Mandy flew after him.

He pulled her inside the gate and slammed the doors shut. "There!" he said, panting. "We're safe in here until it goes away."

Mandy turned to look back. She couldn't see anything, except shadows shifting across the ground. The sound of light footsteps scurrying down the trail made Mandy's fingers quiver as she touched Nick's arm.

"But, Nick," Mandy whispered, 'if it's a ghost dog, can't it come right *through* the gate?"

Chapter 2. The Ghost Dog

Nick stared at her, his face white. "You're right. We'll have to go through the mine and out the other gate." He fumbled just inside the entrance for the light switch. When he flicked it, nothing happened. He moaned. "Great, just great," he muttered. "I don't suppose you have your handy-dandy light with you?"

"As a matter of fact. . ." Mandy pulled a tiny penlight out of her jacket pocket and switched it on. "Here!" she said, thrusting it into his hand. "You know the way better than I do. Let's go!"

They hurried through the tunnel as fast as they could. The gravel floor, packed hard by many feet, twisted and turned into the depths of the earth. Overhead, veins of quartz glistened in the rough, rocky ceiling.

Mandy tried not to think about the tons of rock pressing down over their heads.

The tunnel branched off several times. Nick always chose the left.

"How do you. . . know. . . which way to go?" Mandy asked, gasping out the words.

"Logic!" Nick said back over his shoulder. "The path. . . has to. . . curve left to the. . . other entrance." He tripped over something. "What the heck?" he mumbled, stopping. He shined the light down near his feet. "Whoa, look at this, Mandy!"

The light beam shimmered along a length of chain connected to an iron ring in the wall. The other end of the chain led to a pile of brownish bones.

"Maybe it was one of the miner's dogs," Mandy whispered, her heart skipping a beat.

Nick jumped back as if his feet had been burned. "Crikey!" he cried. "This was never here before!" He backed away from the bones even further. "We must have taken a wrong turn."

"What?" Mandy demanded. "You got us lost? So much for logic!"

"It *seemed* to make sense," Nick said.

"Great," Mandy replied. "Now we have to figure out how to get out of here. Isn't the path the tour takes marked in some way?"

"Usually there are electric lanterns," Nick said, thinking, "but for some reason, they're not working right now." He played the light over the bones again.

"Wait, Nick," Mandy said. "Shine the light on the chain again. I think there's something else there."

She knelt down to get a closer look as the beam of light followed the chain from the ring in the wall to the floor. "There!" she said, pointing to a piece of leather that must have once been a dog collar. The chain was looped around it. Gingerly, she separated the leather from the chain.

"Look, Nick," she whispered. "A key. . . it must have been attached to the dog's collar."

"Wow," said Nick. "I bet it belonged to one of the old miners. I wonder what it opens? Maybe he hid a strongbox full of gold somewhere!"

Mandy picked up the key and rubbed it on her jeans to remove the dust. "Whatever it opened, it must have been important. The dog was guarding it. Do you think it would be okay to take it?"

"That key's been here a long time," Nick said. "The miner is long gone." He glanced around and gulped. "I hope."

"Listen!" said Mandy. "Do you hear that?"

A scratching sound echoed eerily through the tunnel.

"The ghost dog?" Nick whispered. "It's after us!"

He sprinted up the tunnel, leaving Mandy behind.

"Wait, Nick!" she shouted, stumbling after him, barely able to see. She held out her hand so she could feel her way along the rough tunnel wall.

"Hurry up, Mandy!" Nick said from up ahead, his form a sinister silhouette in front of the flashlight.

As the scratching got closer, they could also hear panting, like a dog running fast.

"It's coming!" yelled Nick, taking off again.

Mandy grabbed for the back of his shirt. No way did she want to be left in the dark with that *thing*. "Faster, Nick!" she urged. Frosty breaths seemed to be chilling the back of her neck.

Nick stopped short and Mandy crashed into him.

"Uh, oh," he said. He played the light over the solid rock wall in front of them. "Dead end."

"I *hate* that expression," whispered Mandy.

Clutching each other, they turned to face the approaching ghost dog.

Chapter 3. Lost in the Mine

With their backs to the wall, Mandy and Nick peered into the darkness, afraid of what they would see. They waited for what seemed like an eternity, but nothing happened.

"Okay," said Mandy, taking a deep breath. "I think it's gone – whatever it is. We need to find our way out of here."

"Crud," Nick said, his arms wrapped around himself. "Do you think it's waiting for us?"

"Well, we can't stay *here* all night," Mandy replied. "We'll have to take the chance."

Nick pushed himself away from the wall. "We have to go back the way we came?"

"I guess we do," Mandy replied. "There's no other way."

"Uhh, *you* take the light," said Nick. "After all, it's yours."

Mandy rolled her eyes. *Big chicken*, she thought. *Sometimes he's such a coward.* She didn't feel much braver herself, but she took the penlight and led the way back down the tunnel. She thought about ghosts. Could they actually hurt people or just scare them to death?

Soon they arrived back at the ghost dog's bones.

"Nobody home," Nick joked with a nervous laugh.

"Yeah," said Mandy. "He's still out roaming the mine, looking for lost tourists to haunt."

"Did you *have* to say that? *We're* the lost tourists!"

Mandy studied the bones. "I wonder what kind of dog it was."

"Does it matter?" said her cousin. "It was obviously a huge, ferocious one, probably part wolf. It sure wasn't lovable, big, red Clifford. Do you think we could continue this discussion later and get going?" A sheen of sweat gleamed on Nick's forehead, even though it was cool in the mine.

"Okay," said Mandy. "So if you took a left every time there was a fork, then we should take a right every time going back. Right?"

"If you say so," Nick replied. "Let's just *go!*"

With the penlight thrust out in front of her, Mandy headed down the tunnel with Nick on her heels. At the next fork, she veered right. At the second fork, she turned right again. And then she stopped.

"This doesn't look familiar at all, Nick," she said. "Look, there's some kind of bridge." Mandy shined the light on a rickety wooden structure. "Should we cross it?"

"I don't think so," said Nick. "It would only get us more lost. Plus it doesn't look very safe. What's down there?"

Mandy inched closer to the bridge and aimed the light over the side. It showed another tunnel far below, far enough to break your neck if the bridge collapsed. She backed away from the edge, bumping into Nick. "Shoot," she said. "How many tunnels are there in this place anyway?"

"Dad says there are seven different levels. When the vein of quartz ore ran out in a tunnel, the miners would start digging a new one either above or below the old tunnel."

"Well, that's just ducky," said Mandy. "We're like rats in a maze. We could be running around in here for days before we find our way out!"

"No," Nick said, his eyes wide. "We *have* to get out. This place is really getting to me. Let's back up and take the left tunnel."

"Whatever," Mandy mumbled.

They backtracked and took the other turn.

"This *has* to be it," Nick said. "There's no other way."

The two children stumbled down the passageway. They passed an old rusty lantern wedged into a hollow in the rock.

"I wish that lantern worked," Mandy said.

"Why?" asked Nick. "We've got a light."

"Would you happen to have a spare battery?" Mandy asked in a tight voice.

"You're kidding, right, Mandy?" Nick babbled. "Please tell me you're kidding."

The light dimmed and went out.

Chapter 4. A Ghostly Voice

The children stood frozen in the total darkness. It was like being buried alive, deep and dark as a tomb.

"Now what?" Nick squeaked.

He clutched Mandy's arm and she could feel him quivering. "We'll just keep following the tunnel," she said, determined to be brave. With her hand against the wall, she scuffed along, her cousin still clinging to her.

"What if there's another fork and we don't know it?" Nick asked.

Mandy hadn't thought of that. In the dark they would be unaware of any tunnels branching off. She stopped in her tracks. "I know," she said. "Let's hold hands. You run your other hand along the wall on that side and I'll touch this side."

"Hold hands?" said Nick. "Gross!"

"Do you have a better idea?" Mandy demanded.

Nick was silent for a moment. "So if we run into a rock wall, we'll know we've come to a fork. Do you have a helmet handy?"

"Just take it slowly," Mandy said. "We'll be okay."

Nick grabbed her wrist instead of her hand and, one step at a time, they inched down the tunnel.

Mandy had experienced total darkness only once before – in the underground tunnel below the farmhouse in New Hampshire. She blinked her eyes a few times to be sure they were open. It was like being blind -- your eyes open but seeing nothing. She shivered and closed them. At least that felt more natural. When you have your eyes shut you expect it to be dark.

Nick's grip on her wrist tightened. "Did you hear something?" he asked.

They both stopped and listened.

"Nick. . . Mandy," an eerie voice floated through the passageway.

"Crikey," whispered Nick. "Does the ghost dog know our names?"

"Shh, listen," Mandy said, opening her eyes.

"Nicholas-las-las," the voice echoed.

"It wants *me*!" Nick plastered himself against the wall. "We have to hide!"

"You can't hide from a ghost, Nick," Mandy said. "If it *is* a ghost."

"What do you mean?" her cousin asked, panic in his voice. "Of course it's a ghost. . . and it's coming to get me!"

"Where are you-you-you?" The voice seemed to be a little louder.

"Oh, no," Nick moaned, shrinking against Mandy. "I'm doomed."

"Hello?" Mandy called out.

"No, Mandy! What are you doing?" Nick sputtered.

Mandy wasn't sure if her eyes were playing tricks on her, but it looked like there was a tiny bit of light in the tunnel. She held her free hand in front of her face. Yes, she could just make out the shape of it, darker than the wall behind it.

"Someone's searching for us, Nick," she said, giving him a shake.

"That's what I'm afraid of," he said in a creaky voice. "Why are you calling to it?"

"Snap out of it, Nick," Mandy said, shaking him again. "It's a human. I think it's your dad."

"Huh?" Nick said. He released the death grip on her arm.

A glint of light in the distance caught their attention. As it moved toward them, the walls and rocky floor of the tunnel became visible again.

"Uncle Ross? We're here!" shouted Mandy. She started walking toward the light.

Nick hung back.

"Come on, Nick," Mandy said. "We're safe. We've been rescued."

"Right," Nick mumbled. "I think I prefer the ghost. Now I'm *really* in trouble."

Chapter 5. The Ghost Dog's Key

"Nick! Mandy! Are you all right?" Uncle Ross held a lantern high so that the light spilled down on them.

"We're okay, Dad," said Nick, shielding his face from the bright glare.

His father's worried expression turned to a scowl. "You've got some explaining to do, Nick. What on earth possessed you to go into the mine alone? You know it's dangerous in here! You could fall down a hole or get trapped by a cave in."

He'd never believe us if we told him, Mandy thought. *Ghost dog? Right.* "Uh. . . there was a coyote after us," she said, since Nick seemed to be speechless. "We thought we could go in one gate and out the other, but we uh, kind of got mixed up somehow."

"We'll talk about this later," Uncle Ross muttered, "after I've had a chance to calm down. Come on." He turned and stalked back up the tunnel.

Mandy glanced at her cousin. He was staring at the ground as they trotted along the passageway, trying to keep up with his father's angry strides.

"I'm dead meat," Nick whispered. "Dad will probably *throw* me to the coyotes!"

At the house, Uncle Ross flicked on the kitchen light. "Mandy, will you rustle up some sandwiches while I have a private word with Nick? Everything's in the fridge. Your Aunt Ariel and Christianne will be arriving soon so make a few extra. We'll be back shortly."

"Sure, Uncle Ross," she said, as he led Nick out of the room. "Uh, oh, he's in for it now," she murmured. She spread mayonnaise on pieces of bread and slapped on slices of turkey and cheese. She cut the sandwiches into triangles and stacked them on a plate.

When they returned, Nick sat down at the table, his face flushed.

"You two go ahead and eat, if you want," Uncle Ross said. "I need to figure out what happened to the lights in the mine. There must be a short circuit somewhere." He grabbed the lantern and went out.

"Are you okay?" Mandy asked her cousin, moving the plate closer to him.

"I don't feel like eating," Nick said, pushing the plate away. "Dad was as mad as a wigged out wasp, saying how irresponsible I am and how I put you in danger with my reckless behavior." He reached past her to grab a sandwich. "I'm such a failure," he mumbled, taking a bite.

"Don't be silly, Nick. Your dad was just worried. Parents always act mad after they find out you're okay." She nibbled on a sandwich. "I'm glad he found us. We could still be wandering around in there. . . Do you have the key?"

Nick fumbled in his pocket and pulled out the key from the ghost dog's collar. He laid it on the table. It was kind of rusty and about four inches long with a double tooth and a flat rounded top pierced by a small hole.

Mandy picked it up to look at it more closely. "Nick," she said, "it's got the number 26 stamped into it. I wonder what it opens?" She laid it back on the table.

"My guess is the miner who owned the dog had some valuables stashed somewhere," said Nick. "What safer place to keep the key than tied to the neck of a vicious dog? It must have been well hidden under the dog's collar so someone wouldn't just shoot the dog and take it."

"So what do you think happened to the miner?" asked Mandy with a shiver. "He wouldn't have left the key there after the dog died, unless. . ."

"Unless he died, too," Nick finished. His sandwich stopped halfway to his mouth. "That means. . ."

"That the box with his valuables is still out there!" Mandy said in an excited voice. "Treasure, Nick, treasure!"

Just then the door flew open. "Mandy!" Christianne yelled, hurrying over to the table and flinging her arms around her cousin. "I'm so glad you're here!"

"It's good to see you, little cousin," Mandy said, returning the hug. "You're getting pretty tall for an eight-year-old."

Christianne smiled at her and then stared at the key on the table. "Did I hear you say 'treasure'? Did you have an adventure without me?" she asked, suspicion in her voice. "What does the key go to?"

"Uh, we don't know that. . . yet," her brother said, sliding the key back into his pocket. "Have a sandwich."

Christianne took a sandwich from the plate. "Where did the key come from?"

"We found it in the mine," Mandy explained. "Connected to a dog's collar."

"A *ghost* dog," Nick emphasized.

The little girl's eyes shone with excitement. "A ghost dog? Oh, boy! Remember, we ghost hunters have to stick together! I want to help find the treasure."

"We don't even know if there *is* a treasure," said her brother, but his eyes locked with Mandy's. They were both thinking the same thing.

There *had* to be a treasure. . . somewhere in that deep, dark place. The question was how could they find it if they were forbidden to go into the mine alone?

Chapter 6. An Alien Place

"This is a very cool place," Mandy said the next morning. She wandered round the main room of the tour center's museum, a building next door to Nick's house, gazing at wild animal heads mounted high on the walls. Below them was a cluttered collection of old mining stuff and lots of old photos from when the mine was active. She stopped to look at one of the pictures. "Just think, Nick. One of these miners could have been the one who owned the key."

Nick peered at the group picture of the rough, scraggly miners. "How will we ever find out who it is? There were so many of them."

"We know he died suddenly," said Mandy, deep in thought. "He didn't have time to unchain his dog." She shivered, thinking about the ghost dog panting through the endless tunnels forever, searching for his lost master.

Nick picked up a chisel and hammer. "This is what they used to make holes in the rock. One man held the chisel while his partner pounded. Once the groove got deep enough, they would roll up some gunpowder in paper, tamp it in with a stick, light the fuse and run."

"Sounds dangerous," Mandy said. "I bet there were a lot of accidents. . . like if they didn't run fast enough." Her stomach felt a little queasy at the thought. "Is there a cemetery? We should check it out." For a moment, she thought about the last cemetery they had visited together behind the haunted farmhouse in New Hampshire. That place had been *full* of surprises.

Nick set down the tools and picked up a chunk of quartz ore. Little bits of silver sparkled in the whitish rock. "Yeah, there's one up the road. But not many people had a headstone. There are some old wooden crosses, but all the names have probably faded away. They've been there for over seventy years."

"Mandy, come see this!" interrupted Christianne, tugging on her arm. "You won't believe it!"

Mandy followed her toward the back of the building. They stopped in front of an open door. Mandy jumped back, a hand over her heart. "Good grief!" She stared at a family of aliens sitting on the bed, who stared back at her. "I sure didn't expect that!" she exclaimed. "Creepy." A hand on her shoulder jumped her again. She whipped around, ready to fend off another alien, but it was just Nick.

"North of here is State Route 375," he said, "a road that goes right across Nevada. When people are driving there at night, they sometimes see UFOs. It's actually called the Extraterrestrial Highway!"

Christianne's blue eyes were big as flying saucers. "If we go there, maybe we can see ET," she said. "He could take us to his planet."

"But he might ask to use your cell phone to call home," her brother said, rumpling her hair.

"I don't have a cell phone," Christianne replied.

Nick rolled his eyes. "Never mind. Let's get going. Dad gave me a list of things for us to do today. First off, he wants us to feed the horses."

"You have horses?" Mandy asked, her eyes sparkling. "Wow! Let's go."

The stable consisted of a corral with a metal roof over part of it for shade and shelter. Bales of hay were stacked outside the fence. Nick threw a couple of bales over the rail and then scooted under the fence to remove the string and spread the hay around. The horses ambled over –

two tall bays, a paint pony, a plump dappled gray, a sleek appaloosa and a palomino. They gathered round the broken up bales and snatched mouthfuls of hay.

"They're beautiful," said Mandy, reaching out to pat the white mane of the appaloosa. "Why do you have so many horses?"

"They're not ours," explained Nick. "Dad and his boss take tourists out on trail rides. He said the mine tours by themselves wouldn't earn enough money. They also rent out kayaks and canoes."

Mandy looked around at the dry, dusty landscape surrounded by dry, dusty hills. "Where's the water?"

"Down this road a couple of miles," said Nick, pointing in the direction of the hazy purple mountains of Arizona, "is the Colorado River. We put boats in where the landing used to be for shipping the gold and silver from the mines. Upstream is the Hoover Dam. Of course, the dam wasn't there back in the old days."

His sister, bored with the history lesson, stuck her hand in his pocket and took out the list. "So what does Dad want us to do next?" she said, trying to decipher her father's writing.

Nick snatched the list from her hand. "A group is coming at ten. He wants us to saddle the horses for them and then go on the mine tour afterward. Dad now thinks it would be a good idea for us to learn our way around the mine better. Not that he wants us in there alone." He stopped to grimace at Mandy. "But he says it's 'just in case.'"

"Just in case what?" Mandy asked, still stroking the appaloosa's neck.

"Um, maybe something unexpected, like last night? Dad's only been working here a month, so I've been in the mine just twice, not counting our visit last night. Anyway, it will give us a chance to get another look. . . with the lights on." He kicked around two more bales of hay for the black mare and chestnut gelding that wandered over to the feeding area.

Nick showed Mandy how to saddle a horse, positioning a saddle pad and then hefting a heavy western saddle onto the palomino's back and tightening the cinch. Each saddle and bridle had the horse's name written on it with permanent marker. He took the bridle labeled Taffy, fit the bit into the horse's mouth and then looped the reins over a post.

Mandy slid a saddle off the fence and lugged it over to Nick. "Circus," she panted. "Which one is that?"

Her cousin pointed to the spotted appaloosa. "Your favorite," he said. "Here, I'll get that for you." He grabbed it from her and settled it on the horse's back. "Pull the cinch tight," he said, "but after the rider gets on, we have to tighten it again. The horses like to play a trick – they blow up their bellies like a balloon when they're being saddled. Later, when they relax, the cinch will be too loose and the seat could slide down."

Mandy giggled at the thought of all the riders hanging upside down from their saddles. "It would sure give you a different view of things." She found Circus' bridle and handed it to Nick.

Like a pro, he slid the bit in and buckled the straps. He led Circus to the fence.

Christianne, too small to saddle horses, amused herself by pulling tufts of hay from the stack of bales and hand feeding them to the other horses.

Nick stopped with a saddle for the paint pony in mid-air. "Christianne," he hissed. "Don't move!" He dropped the saddle into the dust and picked up an empty metal bucket. *"When I count to three, I want you to jump up on the fence as high as you can."*

"Why?" the little girl asked in a puzzled voice.

"Just do what I say!" Nick said, beads of sweat on his forehead. "One, two" – he threw the bucket over the fence and it landed with a clatter – "THREE!"

Chapter 7. The Mysterious Shadow

Christianne clambered up to the highest rung of the fence and then glanced over her shoulder. "You missed," she told her brother.

"I wasn't trying to hit it, I was trying to distract it!" he shouted. "Do you realize how close it was to you?"

Mandy stared at Nick, not understanding the alarm in his voice. Why was he yelling at Christianne? Then she noticed movement against the loose hay on the ground at the base of the stack of bales. A long tan S-shape with diamond-shaped patches of brown down its body wriggled across the hay and into the scrub brush beyond the stable. "Snake!" she screamed and jumped up onto the fence, too.

"It's okay," Nick said, "it's gone now. I'll have to tell Dad there's a rattler around. Not good for business if a tourist gets bitten."

"Rattler?" asked Mandy in disbelief. "As in *rattlesnake*? Nick, you didn't tell me there are rattlesnakes in Nevada!"

"Well, you never asked," her cousin said. "Of course, we have rattlesnakes. This is the West. You just have to look where you step."

"I'll never step on the ground again!" she cried, holding onto the fence for dear life. "I want to go home!"

Christianne shinnied her way along the fence until she sat beside Mandy. "Please don't go home," she pleaded. "We won't let the snake hurt you, will we, Nick?"

"Really, we hardly ever see one," Nick assured her. "Like I said, you just have to be careful. . . come on, we need to get the rest of the horses saddled. It must be close to ten." He picked up the saddle from the dirt and plopped it on the horse's back. "Dad will be mad if the horses aren't ready."

Mandy let herself down from the fence, her glance darting around her feet. She pulled on the cinch and then found the paint's bridle. She felt safer close to the horse.

By the time Uncle Ross escorted a family of four to the stable, all sporting new cowboy hats, the horses were lined up and ready to go. He introduced them as the Forsythes from Virginia. He got the man, woman, and two kids mounted and scurried around adjusting stirrups and girths. "Mandy, why don't you join us?" he said. "You'll find it interesting. Nick, would you ride caboose?"

"What about me?" Christianne said, pouting. "Where's *my* horse?"

Her father swung her up on the saddle in front of him. "I'll drop you off at the house. Your mom needs your help getting ready for the barbecue."

Mandy was thrilled to be riding Circus. She patted his neck. "Good boy," she said in a low voice and the horse twitched his ears as if listening to her. "You'll protect me from snakes, won't you?" On the other hand, what did horses do when they encountered a snake? Tromp it to death? Run? "Don't think about it," she said through gritted teeth.

In single file, with Uncle Ross leading and Mandy and Nick bringing up the rear, the riders swayed to the rhythm of the horses' clopping hooves. After they had dropped off Christianne at the house, they crossed the road and followed a trail that wove back and forth up a hillside.

Uncle Ross called back over his shoulder, "This path was once used by the ore carts from the mine. They were hauled by mules down to the river." He pointed in the same direction Nick had, down the canyon toward the invisible Colorado River. "Eldorado Canyon got its name from the Spanish explorers who spent many years searching for Eldorado, the fabled city of gold. Of course, there was plenty of gold here, if you knew how to get to it."

The track wound through scrubby-looking bushes and mounds of gray-green foliage topped with yellow flowers. Some hot pink blossoms on a low-growing cactus caught Mandy's eye. "Prickly pear," she said under her breath," just like the picture postcard Nick sent me at Christmas time." How could something so homely-looking produce such beautiful flowers? She had a feeling the desert was full of surprises, some good and some not so good. She reminded herself not to think about snakes.

"Hey, Mandy," Nick said in a low voice. "Look over there by that Joshua tree." He pointed at a bush of gnarly branches with a green tuft at the end of each limb.

Blending in with the tan and gray gravel around it, a small creature with long ears sat watching them. "Jack rabbit," said Nick. "Keep yours eyes open and you might see a bighorn or a fox."

"No coyotes, I hope," Mandy said with a shudder.

"No worries. They come out mostly after dark," Nick said.

"*Mostly?*"

"Well, you never know," her cousin said. "Wild animals don't always follow the rules."

"So where are they in the daytime then?" Mandy demanded.

Nick thought for a minute. "Um, gee, I don't know." He looked kind of surprised that he had never wondered that himself.

"Well, I think I know where at least one hangs out," Mandy said, staring up the hillside. Out of the corner of her eye, she had glimpsed a pale shape disappearing into the black hole of an abandoned mine entrance. She shook her head. Did she really see it or was her imagination playing tricks on her? And was it a real coyote or was it the. . . ghost dog?

Chapter 8. Trouble on the Trail

"Did you see that, Nick?" Mandy asked, still staring at the mine opening as her horse ambled up the trail.

"Huh? See what?" her cousin asked.

"Something went into that black hole over there," Mandy said, pointing. "Maybe a coyote or maybe. . .something else."

"No, I didn't see anything except the rabbit," Nick replied. "But I'm sure lots of animals probably go into the mines to cool off and sleep during the day. In fact, Dad told me about a mountain lion that hangs out in a cave further up the canyon."

"Oh, joy," Mandy muttered under her breath. Something else to worry about.

They were now passing through a 'forest' of strange-looking cacti with light green twisty arms studded with spines.

"What are those called, Nick?" Mandy asked. "They look so soft."

"Don't touch them," Nick warned. "Don't even get *near* them. That's jumping cholla and it lives up to its name. Somehow the needles seem to jump right onto you. I learned that the hard way."

Mandy felt a sudden yearning for home where everything was familiar and safe. Sure, Maine had a few mountain lions, bobcats, bears, and even coyotes, but they pretty much stayed in the woods where they belonged. This place was different – you never knew what might jump out at you and bite, sting, or scare you. She resolved to always be on guard.

"Uh, oh," Nick said, as the line of riders came to a halt. "Something's up."

Uncle Ross was talking on his cell phone with eyebrows knit into a frown. After he closed the phone, he spoke with Mr. and Mrs. Forsythe and then made his way back to Nick.

"Emergency down below," he said. "A tourist had a seizure of some kind in the mine. They need my help. Take the group on up to the top and then down to the spring and wait for me there. Can you do that, Nick?" He gazed at his son with doubt in his eyes.

Nick gulped and then said, "Of course I can, Dad. . . you can trust me. I'll take care of everything. . . don't worry about a thing."

His father nodded. "Good." He handed him the phone. "I'll be back as soon as I can." He clucked to his horse and began a quick descent of the hill, slipping and sliding on the loose rock.

"Okay," Nick said, taking a deep breath and straightening in the saddle, "you ride caboose now, Mandy. Just stay away from those jumping cholla," he added with a lopsided grin.

Mandy watched her cousin ride to the front of the line and lead the group on. It seemed like poor Nick was always disappointing his father. She crossed her fingers, hoping everything would go okay this time.

The trail got steeper and rockier. Mandy clung to the saddlehorn and leaned forward to help Circus up the side of the canyon. She breathed easier when they crested the top. "Oh, wow," she whispered.

Mile after mile of hills stretched out in front of them. The Colorado River sparkled in the sun like a ribbon of silver and beyond that rolled the hazy blue mountains of Arizona.

"It's seven miles to the river," Nick, in tour guide mode, explained to the group.

"Down there is Nelson's Landing where the steamboats docked. They brought supplies for the mining camps and then were loaded with ore from the mines."

"Is there anything there now worth seeing?" asked Mr. Forsythe.

"Well, the dock and all the buildings are gone," replied Nick. "But it's a great place to launch kayaks and canoes to explore the river. You can rent those from us, if you want to try it out."

He's doing a great job, Mandy thought. His dad should be proud. The woman handed Nick a camera and he maneuvered his horse to take a picture of the tourist family with the view behind them. They will treasure that photo forever, Mandy thought with a smile.

After a few minutes of gazing at the amazing scenery, the group started down the other side of the hill.

"Now you want to lean back in the saddle," Nick directed, "and let your horse pick its way down. They've done this a million times so just trust them."

The whine of engines drowned out Nick's words. Two ATVs roared up the hillside with a billowing cloud of dust behind them. They headed right for the horses. Startled, the horses whinnied and swerved away from them. The two helmeted men on the ATVs laughed and barreled on up over the top.

Nick shook his fist at them. "Idiots!" he yelled.

"Who was that?" Mandy asked, glad that Circus and the tourists' horses all stopped when Nick's did. No one had fallen off, thank goodness.

"I don't know," her cousin replied, "but they're crazy! Someone could have been hurt." He took a deep breath. "Okay, everyone, sorry about that. Let's continue our ride."

Nick led them down to an area where a stream chuckled over the rocks, its banks fringed with small trees and even some grass. "Shh, look there," Nick said, pointing. Across the stream on a flat rock, a red fox sat sunning itself. Hearing their approach, its ears perked up and then it slid away into the bushes. "Okay, so we'll take a break here," Nick said. He dismounted and let his horse graze on the sweet grass. He held each of the horses while the tourists got off. "Pull up a rock," he said as a joke, 'and have some chow. Just, uh. . ." He hesitated and glanced at Mandy. "Look out for snakes."

Mandy glared at him. "I'll eat right here," she said, staying on Circus.

He grinned at her. "Suit yourself." He unpacked the saddle bags and passed out granola bars, small bags of chips and bottles of water to everyone.

Just as Mandy bit into her granola bar, she heard a low rumble like a giant grumbling. She glanced at the bright blue sky. Could it be thunder? Her eye caught movement part way up the cliff side. Boulders, large and small, tumbled down, headed right for them.

"Avalanche!" she screamed.

Chapter 9. ⛏ Disappearance in the Mine

Mrs. Forsythe screamed and threw her arms around her children. The whole family stared at the tumbling rocks with horror and fascination.

The horses raised their heads and, before the first boulders hit the stream, they whinnied, wheeled away from the water and galloped down the canyon.

Circus, reacting with the same panic, raced after them. Mandy dropped her food and clutched the saddle horn. With one hand, she snatched the reins and pulled hard. "Whoa!" she yelled. "Stop!"

But the horse ignored her. "Help!" she shouted. "Help, Nick!" She gave up and just held on as the runaways, like a herd of spooked mustangs, galloped together in a cloud of dust.

The horses zigzagged along a trail they knew well and came out on the road. They slowed to a trot, heading back to the safety of the stable. Mandy bounced in the saddle, her teeth clacking together. "Whoa, Circus, whoa!" she said, pulling on the reins again. Finally, outside the corral, the horse stopped, his sides heaving.

Over by the mine entrance, Uncle Ross stood by an ambulance, watching a man being loaded into the back. He glanced up, saw Mandy and the riderless horses, and hurried over. "Mandy, are you all right? What happened?"

"We were eating at the spring," she panted," and rocks started falling down. . . and the horses took off!"

His eyebrows shot up. "Is everyone okay?"

"I don't know," she replied. "I was still on Circus and he ran after the other horses."

"Okay," he said, helping her down. "You run up to the house and tell your Aunt Ariel what happened. I need to get out there fast!" He rounded up the horses, put them on a lead, and cantered off toward the spring.

A half hour later, everyone returned, unharmed. The Forsythes chattered about their close call. "That boulder was as big as a car!" said the boy. "It landed right where that girl on the horse had been standing.

Startled, Mandy realized he was talking about her. Good grief. She and Circus could have been pancakes!

"That boy of yours is a quick thinker," said the man. "He herded us under a rock overhang that protected us from the worst of the avalanche. Thanks, Son," he said to Nick.

Nick blushed and nodded.

Uncle Ross looked at Nick for a moment and gave him a quick pat on the back. "Do you still want the tour of the mine at 1:00?" he asked the tourists.

"Oh, yes," the woman exclaimed. "We wouldn't miss it. This is such an interesting place."

"Yeah, never a dull moment," Mandy muttered to herself.

After enjoying the barbecued chicken, corn on the cob and watermelon Aunt Ariel and Christianne had prepared, the group headed to the mine. This time Christianne was allowed to join in.

"You had another adventure without me," the little girl complained. "Why do I miss out on all the excitement?"

Walking behind her in the tunnel, Mandy said, "Believe me, it was an adventure you were lucky to miss. We could have been killed."

"This is my first time in the mine," Christianne said, looking around with interest. "Is this where the ghost dog lives? Do you think we'll see him?"

Nick and Mandy exchanged a look. "We don't know if there really is a ghost dog," he said. "We didn't actually see anything. Come on, we need to catch up with Dad." He took his sister's hand and they all scurried down the long tunnel to catch up with the tour.

Up ahead, Uncle Ross led the group to a spot where a rusty lantern and a bird cage hung from an overhead beam. "First, Indians and Spanish explorers dug for gold and silver in the canyon," Uncle Ross told the tourists. "When American explorers reached the area, prospectors followed. In the 1860s, promising claims drew miners here. The Eldorado mines employed about 300 men."

"Where did the men live?" asked the Forsythe boy.

"They lived in shacks, tents and the boardinghouse, in a town so wild and violent that no lawman would come near it. That's how it got its name – Forgotten Gulch. There were ten saloons and a general store, but no jail."

Mandy thought about all the people who must have died here, going about their daily business and coming to a sudden and unexpected end. Heck, the mine and the town must be full of ghosts!

"What happened to the bird?" Christianne asked, pointing at the cage. "Did it fly away?"

Her father smiled. "I'm glad you asked that. The miners kept a canary in the cage. As long as the bird lived, they knew the air in the mine was good to breathe. If the bird died, they knew they had to get out of here fast."

"Poor birdie," Christianne said.

Nick snorted. "More like, poor miners. Every minute they were in here, they risked their lives."

Ahead, a narrow wooden bridge spanned a deep pit. It was similar to the one she and Nick had seen the night before when they were lost in the mine, only in better shape. Mandy took Christianne's hand and, after the tourists had taken a look, they stood on the bridge together and peered down. Far below, a dim light revealed part of a tunnel on a lower level.

Mandy gulped. It was a *looong* way down. "Uncle Ross," she said, "how did the miners get down there?"

He pointed to a ladder behind her that leaned against the wall, leading up through a shaft to a higher level. "No elevators here," he said with a laugh. "They used ladders to go up or down. See that?" He nodded at a tilted arrow nailed to the beam above them. "Up that ladder is the emergency exit to be used in case of a cave in on this level."

Nick and Mandy exchanged glances.

"That's good to know," Nick said under his breath.

Mandy jumped as a high-pitched scream echoed through the tunnel. At the same moment, she realized Christianne had let go of her hand and was nowhere in sight. "*Christianne*?" she called, panic-stricken. "*Where are you*?"

Chapter 10. The Ghost Miner

"This way!" said Uncle Ross, swinging the light around. "Christianne, where are you? Christianne?" He hurried down the tunnel and disappeared around a bend.

"She was right here a minute ago," Mandy said to Nick. "How could she disappear so fast?" If something happened to her little cousin, she would never forgive herself.

The group followed Nick's father. As they rounded the bend, Mandy caught a glimpse of Christianne backed up against the tunnel wall, crying and pointing at something. Her father rushed up to her, knelt down and hugged her, pressing her wet face against his shirt front.

"It's all right, Christianne," he said. "It's all right."

Mandy gasped when she saw what had scared her cousin. A skeleton, partially covered with wisps of decayed clothing, sat against the rocks behind a black metal fence. A steel chisel had been driven through its skull. "Good grief," she whispered. "What happened to him?"

"It's okay, everybody," Uncle Ross said, "nothing to be afraid of. This is part of the tour. It's an old miner who tamped his gunpowder charge with his chisel instead of a wooden dowel. A spark from the hammer set off the gunpowder and blew the chisel right through the poor guy's head. This has been here a long time."

"Awesome!" said the Forsythe boy.

"That's sick," said his sister.

Their father took some flash photos of the skeleton. "The other miners just left the man's body here?" asked the woman.

"The work had to go on," said Uncle Ross, standing and giving Christianne a nudge toward Mandy and Nick. "Probably the boss thought it would be a good reminder to everyone to not take shortcuts! Plus, the miner was thought to be one of the victims of Queho's Curse. Queho, a notorious renegade Indian, murdered twenty-three people. Everyone in this part of the country feared him."

Mandy held out her hand to Christianne. "Why did you wander off?" she whispered. "You scared the wits out of me. My heart is still pounding!"

"I thought I heard the dog," the little girl said, sniffing. "I wanted to see him."

"What did it sound like?" Nick asked.

"Huh, huh, huh, huh," she huffed like a dog panting. "I think he had been running."

Nick and Mandy stared at each other. They hadn't imagined it. Christianne had heard the same sounds they did. *The ghost dog.*

The tourists thanked Mr. Dorr for their eventful day and headed for their car.

"Race you back to the house!" Christianne said, tagging Nick's arm. The children ran to the front porch with Christianne winning by a nose.

A few minutes later, Mandy swirled the straw in her glass of lemonade with a thoughtful look on her face. "Nick," she said between sips, "do you think that guy in the mine – that skeleton – owned the dog?"

Nick stopped drinking. "Well, it would sure explain why the dog was left to starve to death. His owner died so suddenly, he never had a chance to unchain him."

"Poor doggie," Christianne said, shaking her head.

"And the key must have been hidden under the dog's collar, so no one knew where it was until. . . until we found it,"

Mandy reasoned. "We've got to find out who the miner was."

"But how?" asked Nick. "Remember, Dad said three hundred men worked the mines here in the canyon. How can we identify one out of so many? It's not like they carried a driver's license or ID tags."

"No," said Mandy, her face scrunched up in thought, "but there might be other ways to identify someone. . . We'll have to go back."

"Huh?" Nick said. "Go back where?"

"In the mine," said Mandy, rattling the ice cubes in her glass. "We need to get a closer look at him and any stuff he had with him."

"No, Mandy!" Nick said. "Do you know how much trouble I'd get into if I take you back in there? I'd be grounded for a year!"

"I won't be afraid this time," Christianne said in a determined voice. "An old pile of bones won't hurt anyone." She shivered in spite of her brave words.

"Look, Nick," Mandy said in a low voice. "Something fishy is going on around here – the lights in the mine not working and the dog sounds. We need to get to the bottom of this."

Nick put his head in his hands and sighed. "The avalanche, too. You're right. If things get any more dangerous around here, Mr. Vance will have to stop the tours and Dad will lose his job."

"Plus, if we can find out the name of the miner, maybe we can figure out what the key opens," Mandy said. "It must be important."

"Treasure!" said Christianne, her eyes shining. "We're going on a treasure hunt!"

Nick groaned. He was outnumbered again. "All right," he said, "but this time we'll be prepared with lots of flashlights and something to mark our trail with. And we should bring rope, in case. . ." He gulped. "Well, in case we need it."

"Right," said Mandy. "We'll meet in the kitchen at midnight."

Chapter 11. The Mine at Midnight

The three children tiptoed out of the house, closing the door behind them with a faint click.

"This way," whispered Nick, trying to step lightly so the gravel didn't crunch.

Pinpricks of light pierced the night sky, more stars than Mandy had ever seen before. She recognized the Big Dipper and Draco the Dragon and it gave her comfort to know it was the same familiar sky she knew back in Maine.

A flash of light blazed overhead as a meteorite flared and then fizzled out.

"Wow, a shooting star!" said Christianne, dancing in a circle. "I'm going to make a wish!"

"Shhh!" warned her brother. "Don't get too excited. It might be an alien spacecraft."

"Really?" asked his sister in a whisper. "Is ET coming to visit us?"

Nick snorted. "Why are you so hung up on ET? He's a homely little guy with all that wrinkled skin and those big bug eyes." He turned the key in the lock and pushed open the gate in front of the mine entrance. "As much as I hate to say this, we better not turn on the electric lights. Mom and Dad might see them from the house." He shined his flashlight into the deep, dark hole. "Uh, ladies first."

It was Mandy's turn to snort. "Gee, thanks," she said. "You're such a gentleman." She took Christianne's hand. "Don't you dare let go," she warned the little girl. "I want you to stick to me like glue."

"Elmer's or Super Glue?" asked Christianne.

"*Super* Glue," said Mandy. "Keep holding my hand no matter what."

The children made their way down the long tunnel. Their shadows flickered in an eerie dance on the rough rock walls. At the first fork they stopped.

"Nick, do you remember how to get to the. . . the Old Miner?" Mandy asked. Somehow saying the word 'skeleton' was just too creepy. She flashed the light first down one tunnel and then the other. They both looked the same to her.

"I think we turn left here," her cousin said. "Let's leave a mark so we'll know how to get back." He took a piece of chalk out of his jeans' pocket and drew an arrow on the wall.

"Can I have some chalk?" asked his sister.

"No way," said Nick. "If you start drawing smiley faces and ETs on the wall, Dad will know we've been here for sure!"

She stuck her tongue out at him. "No fair. I never get to do the fun stuff."

Nick sighed. "If you stop complaining, I'll let you draw the next arrow."

"Shh, listen," Mandy interrupted. "Did you hear something?"

Everyone froze. They stared at each other, listening. A faint tapping noise echoed down the tunnel. There seemed to be a pattern -- six or seven taps, a pause, more taps, another pause, over and over.

"What is it?" Mandy whispered to Nick. She saw his Adams apple bob as he gulped.

He stared at her, his face white. "It sounds like s-someone mining. . . the old-fashioned way. Remember how I told you the miners used a chisel and hammer to drill into the quartz? After a few thunks with the hammer, they would rotate the chisel a quarter turn to keep the hole even."

"Who would be mining in the middle of the night?" Mandy asked, not sure she really wanted to know the answer.

"The Old Miner's g-ghost?" said Christianne in a squeaky voice. She squeezed Mandy's hand hard. "Maybe he's still trying to find gold."

"Let's follow the sound," Mandy suggested.

"Let's not," said Nick, but Mandy had already headed down the tunnel with his sister in tow.

When they came to the next spot where the tunnel divided, the tapping was louder. Without speaking, Mandy pointed to the right. Nick handed the chalk to Christianne so she could draw an arrow on the wall. When he tried to snatch it back, she hid it behind her back and stepped sideways.

"Whoa!" Nick shouted as he tripped over a rock and sprawled on the ground. "Ohhh," he moaned. Slowly, he sat up and glared at his sister. "Darn it, Christianne! Now look what you've done." He cupped his skinned elbow.

"Shhh," warned Mandy. "The tapping has stopped."

Still as the stone around them, they listened. A scraping sound like something heavy being dragged across the floor was followed by creaking.

Mandy put a finger to her lips and then beckoned her cousins to follow her.

Tiptoeing down the corridor, they came to a third turn-off. This time Mandy pointed left. Frowning at his sister, Nick held out his hand for the chalk. After he had made his mark, they continued down the left tunnel.

In the gleam of her flashlight, Mandy noticed the bird cage and old lantern from the tour hanging above their heads. A few steps further lay the bridge where they had been standing when Christianne had disappeared. That meant right around the bend was the Old Miner.

The creaking noises stopped. Silence wrapped around them like a sorcerer's cloak. The three children held their breaths. Where there should be only darkness, flickering light cast a strange glow on the tunnel wall.

What would they find around the corner? Was the Old Miner taking a rest from his eternal labor? Or did he hear them coming? Was he waiting for them, hammer raised?

Chapter 12. Cave In!

With their backs plastered against the wall, the children inched their way toward the bend in the tunnel.

Mandy could hardly hear with her heart pounding in her ears. Ready to run at a moment's notice, she peeked around the corner. Christianne and Nick crowded behind her.

On the opposite wall a candle in a metal holder burned with an unsteady flame. By its light, they could see the skeleton of the Old Miner still lying behind the fence. The dark eye sockets stared back at them.

Mandy shuddered. Was the man's ghost hovering unseen in the tunnel? The hairs on the back of her neck prickled with that feeling of being watched.

"Who-oo lit the candle?" asked Nick, his teeth chattering.

They all stared at the flickering flame as if hypnotized.

In her mind, Mandy's thoughts bounced like ping pong balls as she tried to come up with an answer to that simple question. Could a ghost light a candle? Did a ghost even need a light to see? Or was it a real person? If so, why? And where was he now?

"Maybe the aliens are looking for gold," Christianne suggested in a small voice.

That broke the spell. Nick snorted and Mandy smiled.

"We'll think about the candle later. Let's get a closer look at the miner," Mandy said. "Can we get inside the fence, Nick?"

Her cousin took the ring of keys out of his pocket that he had borrowed from the hook beside the kitchen door. He sorted through them, looking for the right key. "This one ought to do it," he said. "It's the only one small enough to fit a padlock." Once Nick had it unlocked, he pulled open the narrow metal gate which screeched in protest.

With Mandy in the lead, the three children sidled into the area around the skeleton. Next to its feet lay a battered pail and a rusty hammer.

Mandy tried not to look at the skull with the chisel sticking out of its forehead. She knelt and aimed her flashlight at the remnants of clothing. It looked like the man had been wearing brown pants and a flannel shirt with a sort of dark green cloth around his neck.

His dusty boots were so worn that a hole had started on both soles. An old felt hat had tumbled off the man's head when he fell and lay upside down on the floor.

"Look at that!" said Christianne, pointing her little penlight at the man's belt. The light picked up the dull gleam of tarnished metal. "Is that his dog? The. . . the *ghost* dog?" she whispered.

Nick added his light to hers, making a bigger circle of illumination. "It's a belt buckle. . . a cool one."

The metal buckle was the shape of a wolf's head with its mouth open in a snarl. Two chips of red stone formed the eyes.

"I'm surprised that buckle is still there," Nick exclaimed. "You'd think someone would have snatched it after the miner died."

"Uh, don't you get the feeling this guy was jinxed?" Mandy said. "Remember the Curse of Queho? I don't think anyone would want to risk taking something of his. The bad luck would pass to them."

"That's silly," Nick said. "Nobody believes in that superstitious junk."

"Oh, no?" replied Mandy. "What about the Hope Diamond? Bad things happened to everyone who owned it. That's why it ended up in a museum. And what about the curse of King Tut? So many died who were responsible for opening his tomb, tons of people thought there was a curse."

Nick still held his light on the buckle, studying it closely. "You know," he said, "this kind of looks familiar. Where could I have seen it before?"

"Now that you mention it. . ." Mandy thought for a moment. "The photos, Nick! The ones we were looking at this morning in the museum. "Wasn't one of a guy standing next to an Indian? And wasn't he wearing a hat and a handkerchief just like these?"

Nick gave a low whistle. "I think you're right, Mandy! We'll have to look at it again with a magnifying glass to be sure."

"If he's in a photo, there might be a name written on it!" Mandy said in an excited voice. "Then we would know who owned the key we found on the dog's collar!"

"Will that help us find the treasure?" Christianne asked, puzzled.

"It would be a clue," replied Mandy, "and one clue leads to –"

A deep rumble, like a giant clearing his throat, interrupted her.

"What's that?" Mandy asked.

A wave of dust rushed at them and the children stumbled back against the wall.

"Cover your mouth and nose with your shirt sleeve!" Nick yelled. "And close your eyes! *Cave in!*"

Chapter 13. Lost!

"Keep your eyes closed until the dust settles. . . and keep breathing through the cloth," Nick's muffled voice said. "Is everyone okay?"

"I – I *think* so," said Mandy through her sweatshirt. "Christianne?"

The little girl coughed. "I don't like this! I want to go home."

"We have to wait until the dust clears," her brother said.

Mandy could tell he was trying to stay calm so his sister wouldn't freak out. Who knew if they would be able to get out at all? If the falling rocks had blocked their way, they were doomed. They would be keeping the Old Miner company for eternity. She shook her head to rid it of such awful thoughts.

"Stay near me, Christianne," she said, reaching for her cousin with her free hand. She opened one eye to just a slit. Dust still swirled around them but it didn't seem quite as thick. The candle had gone out. The flashlight she had dropped lay at her feet, still on, thank goodness. She took Christianne's hand and pulled her close.

After what seemed like forever, Nick said, 'Okay, you can open your eyes now. The dust has pretty much settled down." He took his inhaler from his pocket and took a few deep breaths. Then he picked up his flashlight from the floor and clicked the on-off button a few times. "Great, it's broken." He picked up Mandy's. "So we've got one light left. . ."

"Two," said his sister, drilling him in the eyes with her penlight beam.

"Hey, cut it out," he said, shielding his face. "Let's see how bad this is." He stepped out of the skeleton's fenced-off area and headed back up the tunnel. Then he stopped, playing the light over a tumble of rocks that sealed off the passageway. He groaned and sat down on a boulder. "We're trapped." A drop of sweat rolled down the side of his face. He reached in his pocket for his inhaler.

"I hope you're not giving up already," Mandy told him. "What about the emergency exit your dad mentioned?"

For a moment Nick looked hopeful, then his shoulders sagged. "It's on the other side of the rockslide, remember?"

"Oh. . . right." She was silent for a moment. "Christianne, may I borrow your light for a sec?" she asked.

The little girl handed her the penlight. "Mandy, how do we get out?" she asked in a shaky voice. "Are we going to die?"

Mandy slowly waved the light over the rock slide. She had to be brave for Christianne. She grabbed a stone on top and rolled it down the side of the pile. "Come on, help me," she said to her cousins.

Christianne scrambled up beside her and moved the smaller rocks aside. Nick just groaned and put his head in his heads. "It's hopeless," he muttered.

Soon, the girls had the top of the pile cleared away. Mandy stopped to shine the light around. "Look, Nick!" she exclaimed. "There's an opening in the ceiling! Bring my light up here."

Nick stirred from his misery and dragged himself to where they sat.

Mandy snatched the light from him and aimed it into the black hole above. "It's another tunnel! Where do you think it goes, Nick?"

"Who knows?" he replied in a gloomy voice. "There are miles of tunnels in this mountain. We could wander around like rats in a maze for a century. I vote we stay right here and wait to be rescued."

Christianne whimpered. "I don't want to stay here. I want Mom and Dad."

"I think we should try it," Mandy said. "Uncle Ross won't find us until morning and then who knows how long it will take him to clear the tunnel? It could be days."

"Man, I can't win," said Nick. "I get to choose between being lost in a web of creepy tunnels with ghosts running around or staying here, starving, and getting killed when Dad finally finds me."

"Come on," urged Mandy. "The lights won't last forever. We need to get moving."

She crawled up through the hole with Christianne right behind her. Nick hauled himself up and followed. The ceiling seemed lower in the new tunnel and debris littered the floor, making for slow progress.

"This doesn't look like a way out to me," Nick muttered after awhile.

"Watch your step," Mandy warned, sidling around a rusty ore cart. A few yards further along, she stopped short with a shriek. "Eeek!" She fell back against Christianne and Nick. "Hold onto me!"

"What's the matter?" yelled Nick.

"Another h-hole." Mandy shuddered and clung to Christianne. What a close call. One more step and. . ." She gulped. "Do you still have that rope, Nick?"

He unslung it from his shoulder. "Yeah, why?"

"We – we need to go down," Mandy said. "This opening is too wide to cross and it looks like the tunnel is blocked up ahead anyway. So back up and tie the rope to the ore cart we just passed. Tie it really *tight*, okay?"

She lay on her stomach and peered over the edge, shining her flashlight below. It was a long way down. She hated heights. Once she had climbed an apple tree and couldn't get back down.

She sat in the tree for an hour, yelling for help, before her father came along. He had talked her down, one step at a time.

Nick shimmied back her way and handed her the end of the rope. "Looks like a shaft down to a lower level. Be careful."

She glared at him. "Wait, why do I have to be first?"

"Someone's got to test it out and make sure it's safe. Christianne's too small and I'm the heaviest, so you're elected."

"Right," she said through clenched teeth. She grabbed the rope and slid it around her waist. She tied three knots and then one more, just to be sure. "You'll have to let me down slowly," she said. "Got it? *Sloooow-ly*." She sat on the rim of the hole with her feet dangling over empty space. "Okay. . . ready." She squeezed her eyes shut. Mandy took a deep breath and slid off the edge.

Chapter 14. A Struggle With Fear

Nick and Christianne strained to hold onto the rope, letting it out inch by inch.

Mandy dangled in the mine shaft, not daring to look. From above, it had looked like a drop that equaled the height of a two-story house. Her stomach fluttered with fear. She could hear her cousins grunting with the effort of holding onto the rope. *Please don't let go*, she silently prayed. They let her down in jerky movements. At last her feet touched the ground. With shaking fingers, she fumbled at the knots until she had them untied. She gulped air. "All set. Christianne next!" she called up to her cousins. The end of the rope disappeared up over the edge.

"Give me your light," Nick demanded, taking the penlight from his sister. He set it on a rock so he could see as he wound the rope around her waist and tied it tightly.

"Hey, I can't breathe," she complained. "Are you trying to cut me half like a watermelon?"

"Be quiet," he said. "I'm trying to make sure you won't slip out of the rope and smash your head open like a watermelon."

"Oh." She sucked in a small breath and scooted over to the rim of the shaft. "Ready."

"Close your eyes, Christianne," Mandy shouted, "and don't worry – I'll catch you!"

Nick began to let out the rope and the little girl spun in circles as he lowered her down. When she was close enough, Mandy reached up and steadied her.

"Okay, you're safe," she told her cousin. "You can open your eyes now." She set Christianne on the floor and untied the rope.

"Uh, problem here," Nick said from above. "Who's going to let *me* down?"

"You'll have to slide down the rope," Mandy called up to him. "Like a fireman pole."

"You've got to be kidding!" Nick said. "I can't do that!"

Mandy hid a grim smile behind her hand. It served him right for making her go first. "There's no other choice, that I can see. . . unless you want to go back and sit it out with the Old Miner."

Silence from above told Mandy that her cousin was thinking about his options. Or maybe he was petrified, gripped with terror so strong it twisted your guts and turned you to stone. She knew how that felt and it wasn't funny at all.

"I'll tie the rope to something to make it more stable." She looked around. The only thing solid enough seemed to be a big rusty hook stuck in the wall. She wrapped the rope around it and tied it with a couple of knots. ""Okay, Nick," she said, "you can do this. You've climbed the rope in gym class, right? This is just the same, only easier because you only have to go down."

His pale face peered over the edge. "Yeah, right, a one-way trip to destruction. This rope's a lot skinnier than the one in phys. ed."

"Come on, Nick, you can do it!" Mandy encouraged. "Just grip it with both hands, wrap your legs around and let yourself down a little bit at a time."

"I can't."

"Nick," said Christianne, "I'll give you that giant jawbreaker I got for my birthday. It's too big for my mouth but it will fit in yours."

Nick snorted. "Gee, thanks. Are you saying I have a big mouth?"

Mandy couldn't help herself. "If the shoe fits, wear it."

"All right, you two, you're in for it now!" He eased himself over the rim and started shinnying down the rope.

Mandy grinned at Christianne and gave her a 'high five.' "Good going," she murmured. All Nick needed was to get a little mad.

Nick was nearly three-fourths of the way down when a sudden 'twang' startled them all. The top end of the rope slithered over the edge and down the shaft.

"Ahhhhh," Nick screamed. He plummeted toward the floor of the mine, still gripping the useless rope. "Oomph." He landed right on Mandy and Christianne. They lay in a tangled heap.

"Ooooooh," Mandy moaned. "Get off me, Nick. I can't breathe."

Her cousin sat up. "I'm still alive?"

"Afraid so," she retorted, testing her arms and legs one by one to see if anything was broken.

Christianne crawled out from the pile-up. "Why did you flatten us, Nick?" she asked, rubbing a bruised arm.

"Revenge?" he said with a weak smile. "For calling me a big mouth." The smile disappeared. "Actually, the rope broke. It must have frayed from being rubbed on the edge of the ore cart." He shuddered. "Thank goodness, I wasn't any higher up when it happened."

"I'm glad you're okay, Nick," Mandy said, "but I think we have a new problem."

"Huh? Now what?"

"We don't have a canary, but if we did, I think it would be 'kicking the bucket' in its cage right now."

"Why would a bird kick a bucket?" Christianne asked.

"Because…of…the…bad…air," Mandy said between gasps. "We need to get out of here – *fast*!"

Chapter 15. The Ghost Dog Returns

"Which way do we go?" Nick asked, looking up and down the new tunnel. "We're more lost than ever."

"I don't know!" said Mandy in despair. One way would lead them deeper into the mountain, the other *might* lead them out.

"Wait!" said Christianne. "Do you hear that?"

Everyone stood still, listening. The light footfalls and whining of the ghost dog echoed in the tunnel in front of them.

"Now what do we do?" Nick asked. "We have a ghost after us, too!"

"He wants us to follow him," his sister said.

"Yeah?" Nick said. "How do you know that? Maybe he wants to get rid of us!"

"No," she insisted. "The ghost dog is good. He wants to help us."

Panic bubbled in Mandy's throat like Coke fizz. They *had* to get moving. "She's usually right," she told Nick. "Let's go!" She found Christianne's hand and ran down the tunnel in the direction of the dog noises.

"*Usually*?" Nick said, and then raced after them.

Mandy thought it was strange they didn't seem to get any closer to the ghost dog. The patter of its feet stayed the same distance ahead of them. Maybe it really *did* want them to follow.

They rounded a bend in the tunnel. A ladder leaned against one wall, going up through a hole in the ceiling. They stopped to catch their breath.

"I don't hear the dog now," said Christianne. "He must want us to climb the ladder."

"Oh, no," protested her brother. "I knew this was a wild goose chase. What makes you think that level is any better than this one?"

Mandy held her light steady on the space above the ladder. "I agree with Christianne. I think I see something up there."

"What is it?" Nick demanded. "An elevator? A sign that says 'this way'?"

"You don't need to be sarcastic," Mandy said. "I'm not sure what it is – a wooden structure of some kind? Maybe the air will be better up there."

"Maybe it will be worse!" Nick replied.

Mandy let go of Christianne's hand and started up the ladder. Christianne scampered up behind her.

As usual, Nick was left in the dark. He groaned and followed.

At the top, the girls' light beams zigzagged around the wooden structure.

"I know what this is!" Mandy said in excitement. "This is the bridge! We were standing here this afternoon when Christianne disappeared *and* we passed over it tonight on our way to the Old Miner. He should be right around that corner!" She swung her light in that direction. The tunnel was blocked with rocks.

"This is where the cave in happened!" said Nick. "Somehow we've come full circle. That means if we go the other way. . ."

"We can get out!" finished Mandy. "Let's go!"

They hurried down the tunnel.

Where it split in two, Nick found his chalk mark on the wall. "All *right*!" he shouted. He located the marks at the other two intersections and soon they were barreling down the last stretch of the passageway.

"Air. . . fresh air!" Nick said, as they burst into the open. He sucked in great gasping gulps.

The stars still sparkled in the night sky. The moon had risen higher and looked smaller. Everything seemed so normal.

As Nick fished the keys out of his pocket and locked the gate to the mine, Mandy glanced at the house. She was relieved to see it was still dark. Now if they could get back to their beds without being discovered.

"You go first!" Mandy hissed at Nick.

"Why?" Nick asked in a surprised voice. "I thought you liked being the leader."

"If there are any snakes out here, I don't want to be the one to step on them." Mandy shuddered. Snakes, especially poisonous ones, were a lot worse than anything in the mine, including skeletons, ghosts and cave ins.

Nick snickered. "Here, Snaky, Snaky," he said in a low voice.

Mandy slapped him on the arm. Then she froze. Why was his arm, not to mention the rest of him, glowing?

Moving her head an inch at a time, she looked up. A bright light from the top of the canyon blinded her. She shielded her eyes with her hand. "What *is* it?" she asked.

Nick and Christianne looked up, too, but the blazing spotlight made it impossible to see anything. Then the light blinked off.

Through the spots in her eyes, Mandy thought she saw a shape outlined with small flashing lights. And then that was gone, too.

"Man," whispered Nick in awe, "a UFO!"

Chapter 16. The Curse of Queho

The three children stared at the sky for several minutes, but nothing else appeared.

"It couldn't be a UFO," whispered Mandy. "They don't really exist. . . do they?"

"ET had to go home," Christianne said in a small sad voice. "It's way past his bed time."

"Forget ET," her brother said. "That's just a movie. *This* is real!" He shook his head. "I can't believe it," he murmured to himself. "I saw a real flying saucer."

Mandy gazed at first one cousin, then the other. "Look," she said, "just because we saw a light up there doesn't mean it's an alien spacecraft. There has to be another explanation.

"This is Nevada, Mandy," Nick replied. "Remember, we're *famous* for UFOs."

"I don't know," she said. "I think someone just made that up to get the tourists to come visit. . . anyway, we'd better go in or we'll be in big trouble."

"Yeah, you're right about that." Nick tore himself away from the spot and walked across the road to the house with the girls following. He eased the door open and hung the keys on the rack.

Mandy glanced at the kitchen clock. 3:05 a.m. No wonder she was so tired. Her head spun in lazy circles like a vulture circling its prey. "Goodnight," she whispered to Nick.

She and Christianne tiptoed to their room and pulled the pillows out from under the covers. They had stuffed them there to make it look like people sleeping.

As they settled into bed, Christianne said, "You know what, Mandy?"

"What?" asked Mandy in a sleepy voice.

"The ghost dog saved us. He led us right to the ladder."

Startled, Mandy's eyes flew open. She thought about how they had been hopelessly lost in the mine until they followed the dog sounds. "You are so right, little cousin," she said, "again." Then she dropped off to sleep.

In the morning, the children sat at the kitchen table, eating their breakfast cereal in a drowsy fog. In the light of day, the strange events from the night before seemed like a crazy dream. Mandy found it hard to believe she had been trapped in the mine, gone up and down scary shafts, followed a ghost dog and been blinded by a UFO. It was like being a character in a video game.

A knock on the door jumped everyone. Mr. Vance, Uncle Ross' boss, stuck his head in. "I need Ross!" he said to Aunt Ariel, who was cooking at the stove. "There's been a cave in at the mine! Tell him to grab a pick and shovel and meet me at the entrance in ten minutes."

"Can we do anything to help?" Nick asked.

"Thanks, Nick," said Mr. Vance, "maybe later. First, we need to see how bad it is." He frowned. "If it's a major cave in, it could put us out of business. We can't risk taking people into an unsafe mine. We've sure been hit by a string of bad luck lately – the tourist having a seizure yesterday, the avalanche at the spring, and now this. You'd think there was a curse on the place!" He ducked out the door.

Mandy gulped and stared at Nick. "Uh, oh," she whispered behind the cereal box. "The Curse of Queho? Do you think he is after us for disturbing the body of the Old Miner?"

"Come on, Mandy," Nick said in a low voice so his mother wouldn't hear as she hurried out of the room. "Two of those things happened *before* we went to get a closer look at the Old Miner. Ghosts can do some strange things, but I don't think they can see into the future."

Christianne slurped the last of the milk out of her cereal bowl and set it down with a thump. "Besides," she said, "the ghost dog likes us. He wouldn't let Queho do anything bad to us."

Her brother rolled his eyes. "Let's go take a look at the photos in the museum. Maybe we can find a picture of the miner." He got up from the table and set his bowl in the sink.

In the museum, the children gazed at the photographs displayed on the walls, searching for any resemblance to the Old Miner's clothing and belt buckle. There must have been fifty or more faded pictures on display, most of them of groups of men. Because they were all in black-and-white, it was impossible to tell what color their clothes were.

"Over here," Nick said. "I think this is him." He pointed to a photo of a man dressed in pants, shirt and hat similar to the Old Miner's. A wolf's head buckle adorned his belt. He stood beside an Indian.

Mandy moved in close to read the words written at the bottom of the picture. "Jacob Snow and Queho." She shook her head "That makes no sense. Why would they have their picture taken together if Queho was so bad?"

"Who knows?" Nick said. "Maybe Jacob Snow didn't have a choice. If you crossed Queho in any way, he would give you the 'evil eye' and your days would be numbered."

"What do you mean?" his sister demanded. "Your days would be numbered?"

Nick gulped and pulled a finger across his throat in a cutting motion.

Chapter 17. A Legend Lives On

"What happened to Queho?" Christianne asked in a small voice.

Nick had a faraway look in his eyes. "He lived like a ghost – killing and then disappearing. He had a reputation so bad that a huge reward was offered for his capture, alive or dead. The last person he murdered here in Forgotten Gulch was a woman named Maude Douglas. In the middle of the night she heard noise in the pantry and when she went to investigate, he shot her. Years later, some prospectors found a mummified body in a cave. It looked like the man had been hiding out there. They think it was Queho."

"If they had their photo taken together, maybe Queho and Jacob Snow were friends," Mandy said. "Why would the miner be friends with a murderer?"

Nick stared at the picture. "Would you rather be his friend or his enemy?" He shuddered and turned away from the hypnotizing eyes in the photo.

"Maybe the Old Miner was a murderer, too?" Mandy guessed.

"No," said Christianne, her chin jutting out in a stubborn line. "He couldn't be bad if his dog was good."

Her brother sighed. "Whatever. So, now that we know his name, how is that going to help us? Should we check the cemetery?"

Mandy was thinking hard. "That wouldn't do us much good since we know he was never buried. His skeleton is still in the mine. The Old Miner – I mean Jacob Snow – had to live somewhere in Forgotten Gulch though – either in a cabin or a boardinghouse. Let's have another look at the key, Nick."

Her cousin pulled it out of his jeans' pocket and laid it on top of a glass display case. The three children crowded close to gaze at it.

Mandy studied it with growing excitement. "I have an idea. Let's look for a book -- you know, a sign-in book like hotels used to have before computers. I remember Dad mentioning once how thrilled he was to stay at the Bar Harbor Inn when he was a boy and how the desk clerk wrote his parents' names down in a big book."

"A book?" said Nick. "You've got to be kidding." He gazed around the cluttered room. Random artifacts – old lanterns, a hand-crank telephone, a small safe, pewter cups, horseshoes, chunks of quartz ore and tons of other things – covered every flat surface . "Forget it. It would be like looking for a needle in a haystack."

"We haven't got anything else to do, have we?" Mandy asked. "It won't hurt to look. We'll divide up the room and each search an area."

A dusty stillness filled the museum as the children peered at each pile of stuff, searching for anything that resembled a book. They tried not to move things around – even though it looked cluttered and unorganized, Mr. Vance probably wouldn't want anything shifted out of place.

After an hour of searching, even Mandy was ready to give up. They had found a tattered old Bible and a small book of poems – that was it for books. She rubbed her dirty hands on her jeans and sighed. "It *seemed* like a good idea."

Christianne stepped in from the next room, carrying a big book balanced on her hands. "What about this?" she said, laying it on the glass case beside the key.

Mandy carefully opened the soiled brown cover. Inside, columns of dates, names and numbers were written in faded ink. "Yes!" she whispered. "I think this is it – the registry of the boardinghouse. Look, *'December 13, 1918, Matthew King, Room 5, paid $10,'*" she read from the first page. "Where did you find it, Christianne?"

"In the back room. One of the aliens was sitting on it," said the little girl, "like a booster chair to make him taller."

Nick hooted with laughter. When he could finally catch his breath, he said, "Maybe the aliens stayed at the boardinghouse, too! They heard what a great vacation spot Forgotten Gulch is!"

Christianne and Mandy looked at each other and then frowned at him with narrow eyes.

"Not funny," Mandy said. Sometimes he was so sarcastic. She didn't want him making fun of Christianne. "When was that picture of Jacob Snow and Queho taken, Nick? Was there a date on it?"

Nick snorted a few last times and then walked over to the photo. "October 1919," he said. "It's right beside the names."

Mandy turned pages of the book, being careful not to tear them. "If he stayed at the boardinghouse, it was probably for awhile." She ran her finger down the columns of names, hoping, hoping. Her finger stopped. The name Jacob Snow jumped out at her. To the left of it, *April 23, 1918,* the date he first took a room, was listed. To the right of his name was written *Room 26.* She looked again at the key.

"That's it!" Mandy said, pointing to the '26' on the key. "It was the key to his room! He kept it tied to the dog's collar so no one could get in while he was working in the mine."

"He must have had *something* valuable in his room if he bothered to lock it," Nick said.

"Treasure," Christianne whispered.

Chapter 18. An Unknown Enemy

"Is the boardinghouse still standing?" Mandy asked Nick.

"Just barely," he replied. "It's that rundown building on the edge of town. The roof's caving in and it looks like one blast of strong wind would blow the whole place down."

Mandy closed the book and picked up the key. "Can we get in?"

"Yes," Nick replied, "but it's risky. We're not supposed to go in any of the buildings that haven't been restored. You could get knocked out by a falling timber or break your leg on a punky floorboard." He eyed her determined face. "But that isn't going to stop us, is it? We laugh at danger, we stare into the face of trouble, we run into the jaws of the lion!" His voice sounded kind of wild.

"Can it, Nick," said Mandy. "We'll be careful."

"I've heard *that* before," he said, crossing his arms. "In fact, I've heard it every time we end up in trouble."

His sister danced from foot to foot. "Come on, Nick, don't be such a scaredy-cat. We have to find the treasure!"

"What makes you think there's a treasure anyway? Maybe he just didn't want anyone stealing his extra pair of long underwear."

"Nick, you said yourself he must have locked his room because he had something valuable," Mandy reasoned. "Of course it was such a long time ago, there probably isn't anything there now, but it won't hurt to check it out. Let's do it now."

Dragging his feet, Nick led the way back to the kitchen where he snagged a small key labeled BH from the key rack beside the door. "Padlock on the boardinghouse door," he muttered.

Little puffs of dust rose around the children as they scuffed down the dirt road of the ghost town. Small cabins where most of the miners had lived were scattered here and there in the valley. Mr. Vance had restored a few of them so tourists could see how they originally looked, but most had collapsed into a sad pile of boards.

Mandy wondered how Mr. Vance and Uncle Ross were doing in the mine. It must be dangerous to clear a cave in. You never knew when more rocks might tumble down. She shuddered to think what a close call they had.

"Nick, what do you think caused the cave-in last night?" she asked her cousin. "The tunnel looked so solid and safe."

"I've been wondering that myself. Dad says the parts of the mine we take the tourists through have been reinforced to the nth degree to pass strict safety standards. It seems impossible it could fall down, except in an earthquake."

Mandy scrunched her face into a frown. "Did you hear anything before the cave in? I thought I heard something like a muffled thud."

Nick stopped and stared at her. "Like an explosion?"

"Maybe," she said, staring back at him. "But that would mean. . ."

"That someone blew it up on purpose," Nick finished with a stunned look.

"Remember the tapping? It wasn't the Old Miner's ghost. A real person must have been drilling to set a charge."

"And we walked right into it," Mandy said in a faint voice. "Why? Why would someone do that?"

"I can think of a couple of reasons," Nick said. "Either he is trying to hunt for gold in Mr. Vance's mine *or* he's trying to sabotage the mine to put us out of business. . . or both."

"Good grief, this is serious, Nick. We need to tell your dad."

Nick shook his head. "That means we would have to tell him we explored the mine in the middle of the night. Do you realize how much trouble we would be in? How much trouble *I* would be in? I would be strung up from the rafters! And Dad would never trust me again." A teardrop squeezed out of the corner of his eye. He wiped it away with an angry gesture. "We're going to figure this out ourselves – we've just *got* to!"

Mandy had never heard him sound so desperate. . . or so determined. "Okay," she said. "Let's start with the boardinghouse. Then I think we should take a look at the top of the hill where that bright light came from last night."

Christianne had been listening to their conversation, her eyes wide. "Where the UFO landed?"

"Right," Mandy said in a grim voice. "Let's go."

They jogged the rest of the way to the old boardinghouse. The long two-story building sagged in the middle. Its walls, weathered to a dull gray, leaned inward and its boarded-up windows stared at them blankly. They stepped onto the tilting porch, testing each spot before putting their full weight on it.

Nick turned the small key in the padlock and it disconnected with a click. He lifted the latch and pushed the door. With rusty hinges squealing in protest, the door cre-e-e-aked open.

Chapter 19. A Strange Discovery

"Did anyone bring a flashlight?" Nick asked in a low voice.

Mandy and Christianne crowded into the entrance behind him. They blinked and tried to see in the gloomy room. The open door provided some light, but not enough to reach the dark corners.

"I did," said Mandy, pulling out her ever ready penlight and clicking it on.

"Me, too!" said Christianne, doing the same.

For a moment the two girls played light sabers with their flashlights.

Nick groaned. "Why am I always the one without a light?"

"Because--" started Mandy and Christianne together.

"Never mind," said Nick, raising his hand. "I don't really want an answer to that question. Shine them over here."

The light beams revealed an old wooden desk and chair and, behind them, two rows of pigeon holes for the guests' mail. On the wall, a board covered with hooks held several tarnished keys.

"Yes!" said Mandy. "Those keys look just like ours. It *must* be a room key!"

". . .Twenty-six, twenty-seven, twenty-eight!" said Christianne, counting the hooks. So there must be twenty-eight rooms."

"With two stories, that's fourteen rooms on each floor," said Nick. "So Room 26 must be on the second floor." He eyed the rickety staircase with doubt in his eyes. "I don't know if that will hold us."

"I don't weigh much," said his sister. "I could go up."

"No way!" Nick protested. "If you get hurt, I'll be deader than a doornail!"

"Nails aren't alive," said Christianne, her brows puckered.

"Exactly!" exclaimed her brother.

Mandy sighed. "*I'll* go first. . . as usual." She lifted her foot to the first step. The wooden tread creaked but it held. Mandy continued upward, one step at a time. "It seems to be okay," she said over her shoulder. "Wait until I'm at the top and then send Christianne up."

Nick waited until his sister reached the landing above and then started up the stairs. His heavier weight made them creak even more. He clutched the railing with nervous fingers. "Uh, I don't know if this is a good idea," he said in a tight voice. Halfway up, the section of railing he held collapsed and crashed over the side. "Ahhh!" Nick screamed, letting go just in time. He sat on the stairs, breathing hard. "I *knew* this wasn't a good idea," he murmured.

"You're okay," Mandy assured him. "Stay in the middle and just go slow."

He inched his way up the rest of the steps on his hands and knees. At the top, he slumped on the floor like a quivering lump of jelly. "Why do I listen to you?" he said through gritted teeth.

Mandy just grinned. She shined her light on the nearest door. "Number 22," she read. "We'll have to go down the hall. Be careful." The corridor seemed as dark as the mine. She kept sweeping the light across the floor. "Missing floorboard," she warned, stepping carefully over the gap in front of Room 24.

"Great," muttered Nick. "Missing *brain* is more like it."

"Here it is," said Christianne, focusing her light on the number of the next door. "Room 26!"

Nick tried the doorknob. "It's still locked." He felt in his pocket for the key. "Heck, where is it?" He searched his other pockets.

"I've got it, remember?" Mandy said, slipping it out of her pocket. She inserted it in the keyhole and tried to turn it, but it wouldn't budge. "I thought for sure it was a room key," she said, disappointed.

"Let *me* try," said Nick. "Remember that front door at the farmhouse in New Hampshire last summer? It opened with an old skeleton key. If you didn't do it a certain way, it wouldn't work." He jiggled the key in the keyhole and tried turning it with different amounts of pressure. "Sometimes if you push in on the door a little it helps." With a few rusty squeaks and a click, the key turned. Nick opened the door.

The girls' lights showed a cot against one wall with a thin mattress partly covered by a ratty gray blanket. Next to it stood a chest of drawers with a cracked mirror hanging above it. A rickety wooden chair on the right side of the bed was the only other furniture. A dingy calendar on the wall showed August 1920.

"There's not much here," Mandy commented, "but let's search everything. Uh, you take the bureau, Nick, and Christianne and I will check out the bed." Mandy couldn't shake the vision of opening a drawer and finding a rattlesnake. . . or a scorpion. . . or a tarantula inside. She shuddered. With two fingers, she slowly peeled back the blanket on the cot. Nothing under that, thank goodness.

"Just a few clothes and some odds and ends here," Nick announced, taking each item out of the bureau and checking it over. "A few hankies, some chewing tobacco, an old letter."

"A letter?" asked Mandy. "Let's have a look." She held out her hand and Nick passed it to her. Being careful not to tear it, she unfolded the brittle paper. Mandy read it out loud.

To whom it may concern:
I feel obliged to write this down, so if something happens to me, the record will be set straight concerning a certain Indian known by the name of Queho.

"Queho!" exclaimed Nick. "Wow, maybe we'll find out why he killed all those people!"

"Shh," said Mandy. "Let me read it."

From the time he was a lad, Queho has been shunned by Indian and white man alike because of his mixed blood and the clubfoot he was cursed with at birth. He grew up with a lot of anger and, at times, it caused him to lose his head and do some rash things.

However, as his only friend, I want to say he is not all bad. I know what it is like to be blamed for a crime I didn't commit. In this lawless canyon, he has become a scapegoat for any and all to blame for unsolved crimes, from missing cattle to thefts and mysterious murders. In the case of Maude Douglas, a young boy in her care said her husband is the one who shot her, but who wants to believe the word of a child? Queho was blamed for that death, even though he had no reason to kill her.

I cannot speak up in his defense because no one would believe me and I would probably be tarred and feathered or knifed in the back. I have a family back East which I must always put first.

My friend has been forced to go into hiding as there is a price on his head. I do my best to bring him provisions and give him a few minutes of human companionship when I can.

If you are reading this, it is because something has happened to me. What will become of my friend I do not know. Have mercy in your heart for Queho.

Sincerely,
Jacob Snow

Chapter 20. A Mystery Unlocked

"What happened to Queho after that?" Christianne asked.

"No one ever saw him again," her brother said in a low voice. "In 1940 when the prospectors found the body, they thought he had probably starved to death. He must have got sick and been too weak to leave the cave."

"Oh, no," Mandy said, staring at the letter. "That means that after Jacob Snow died in the mine, Queho had no way to get food or medicine. He never even knew what happened to his friend. He probably thought he didn't care about him anymore."

"Poor Queho," said Christianne. "He must have been so lonely."

Nick took the letter from Mandy and folded it back up. "Anyway," he said, "at least now the world will know the truth about him. We'll have to think about what to do with this letter. Maybe Mr. Vance will put it in the museum."

"Does that mean there's no treasure?" asked Christianne, disappointed. "The Old Miner put the key on the dog's collar just so no one would read the letter?"

Mandy glanced around the small room. "I don't know. I think we should keep looking. He must have earned money from the gold and silver he found in the mine. He sure didn't spend it on stuff, because there's hardly anything here. . . Why do you think no one unlocked the room before this? Didn't the front desk have an extra key?"

"Probably because of the Curse of Queho," said Nick. "People must have thought Jacob Snow died because he crossed paths with Queho. Remember, no one took the belt buckle off Jacob Snow's body. So, who would want to stay in the room of a cursed miner? Room 26 would not be a popular place. Besides, the boardinghouse closed down soon after that when the mine closed. Everyone moved away and the whole place became a ghost town."

"That means we could be the first people to set foot in this room since Jacob Snow!" Mandy said. "We definitely need to be good detectives and look around more."

We should check everything with a fine-toothed comb," Nick agreed, pretending he was holding a magnifying glass to look at his sister's head. "I think I see something wiggling in your hair."

"Cut it out, Nick," said Christianne, taking a step away from him. "And I didn't bring a comb with me. Anyway, what does a detective do with a comb?"

Her brother snorted. "It just means look at things closely. Don't you know *anything*?"

"Yes I do!" she said, lunging back toward him. She put her foot behind his and gave him a push.

"Hey! Oh. . . ouch!" Nick toppled over and landed on the floor, hard. "You little brat!" he said, rubbing his bruised elbow. "I'll get you!" When Nick tried to stand up, one foot crashed through a floorboard. He fell again. "Darn it, Christianne!" He pulled, but his foot was stuck. "I can't get out!"

Mandy and Christianne looked at each other and grinned. "Too bad, Nick," Mandy said. "See you later, alligator!"

"In awhile, crocodile," his sister added. "Don't let the bedbugs bite!"

The two girls headed for the door.

"Wait!" Nick panted. "Don't leave me here!" He struggled some more, but the boards still clutched his foot just like the jaws of an alligator.

"We'll help if you promise to be good to Christianne," Mandy said. "No more name-calling."

Nick growled at his sister.

"Promise?" she said, staying just out of his reach.

He moaned and said through clenched teeth, "Whatever. I promise. Now get me out of here."

Mandy reached into the hole and pulled on Nick's shoelace to untie it. "Just wiggle your foot around until your shoe comes loose."

He shifted his foot first one way, then the other, and finally pulled it free. He then stooped down to retrieve his shoe. As he shimmied it out of the hole, he noticed something underneath. "Hey, there's a box in here!"

A metal container about the size of a tissue box was wedged in the hole below the ragged boards. He lifted it out and wiped the dust off the top of the box with the bottom of his shirt. "Wow, look at the lock on this thing! It must be old!"

"A combination lock?" Mandy said in dismay. "How will we get it open?"

Nick flipped the brass lock up to look at the other side. Dudley Lock Corp, Chicago, Ill. was etched into the back. "Usually, combinations have three numbers and you turn it forward, back and forward. I have one on my locker at school. We'll just have to guess at the numbers."

"I don't even want to *think* about how long it would take to try every possible number combination with 39 numbers to choose from," Mandy said, shaking her head. "We did something like that in math class and we only used four numbers. It made my head spin."

"Maybe the Old Miner left us a clue," Christianne said. "I think he wants us to find the treasure."

Her brother snorted. "Right, Christianne. We didn't even *exist* when he put this box here!"

"Let me see that letter about Queho again, Nick," said Mandy. "Are there any numbers in it?"

Nick picked up the letter from the floor where it landed when he fell. "Just the date," he said, "June 3, 1920. . . Hey, that might work! Let's try 6-3-20." He turned the dial on the lock and then pulled on it. Nothing happened. "Shoot, that wasn't it."

"You would think Jacob Snow would have written the combination down somewhere in case he forgot it," Mandy said. "Too risky to keep it on him, so it must be in this room somewhere. He would want it near the box. We need to look for numbers--"

They all looked around the room.

"What about the calendar?" asked Christianne, pointing. "It's got numbers all over it!"

Mandy unhooked the calendar from the nail on the wall. She flipped the pages, studying each one carefully. When she reached December, she turned back to January. Three dates were circled. "Ohmigosh, little cousin, I think you've done it again! Look. . . January 5, 13 and 25. Try those numbers, Nick!"

The three children crowded around the box as Nick spun the dial. "They might not be in that order," he murmured. "5-13-25, no. . . 25-13-5, no. . . 13-5-25, no, 25-5-13, no. Oh, shoot, now I can't remember what I already tried!"

"Wait!" said Mandy. "Look at these little marks on the calendar beside the dates. The 13 has one mark, the 25 has two, and the 5 has three! That must be the order of the numbers. Try it, Nick!"

Carefully, her cousin lined up each number with the arrow --13 clockwise, 25 counterclockwise, 5 clockwise. With a tiny click, the lock opened.

"Oh, yes!" crowed Nick. "It worked, it worked! Now let's see what's in here."

Chapter 21. Treasure!

Nick removed the lock and opened the lid of the tin box. Two small leather bags lay inside. Underneath them nestled a packet of letters tied with a pale pink ribbon. He picked up one of the bags and loosened the leather cord around its top. "Shine a light in here," he said.

Mandy aimed her penlight down into the bag. "Wow," she breathed. "Coins! Dump them out, Nick."

He emptied the bag onto the bed. A mass of silver dollars jingled and jangled together like musical notes, twenty of them altogether. The children each picked one up to study it more closely.

"I've seen one of these before," Mandy said, "in Uncle Gabe's coin collection. It's called a Morgan silver dollar."

Nick whistled. "1893! That's old. The CC after the date must stand for Carson City. That's here in Nevada. Dad says they used to mint coins there, a long time ago. I wonder what they're worth?"

"Treasure!" said Christianne, her eyes shining. "I knew it! What's in the other bag?"

Her brother lifted the second bag from the box. "This one's a lot lighter. I'll dump it on the bed, too."

"Wait, Nick," warned Mandy. "Let's see what it is first."

He untied the bag and she aimed the light inside. "It looks like some kind of yellowish powder, maybe corn meal? Better not dump it out," she said.

Nick peered into the bag. He gulped and whispered, "That's not cornmeal. It looks like – like *gold* dust. Oh, man!"

"Let me see, let me see!" Christianne demanded. Her eyes widened as she stared into the bag at the glowing powder. "Wow! We're rich! We're rich!"

"Don't get too excited," Nick said, closing the bag tightly with the leather strip. He scooped up the silver dollars and dropped them back into the other bag. "Even though we found the treasure, it's actually Mr. Vance's property."

Christianne pouted. "Oh," she said, "that's not fair." Then she brightened up. "Maybe he'll let us keep a silver dollar each?"

"Maybe," her brother replied. "It probably depends on how valuable they are." He started to put the bags back in the tin box.

"Wait," said Mandy. "Let's take a look at the letters. Who knows what else we might find out?" She lifted them out of the box, untied the ribbon, and shuffled through the pile. All the letters were addressed to *Jacob Snow, Forgotten Gulch, Eldorado Canyon, Nevada*. Mandy slipped one of the letters out of its envelope and started reading to her cousins.

My dearest Jacob,

How I miss you and long for the time when we can be together again. Every moment of the day I think of you and wonder what you are doing. I worry about you so, working in that dangerous mine. I know we need the money to be able to start a new life in California, but it is taking much too long. Our little Jacob is already two and he has never seen his father!

Please send for us soon. It doesn't matter if we are poor – I just want us all to be together.

Your loving wife,

Olivia

Mandy's voice softened with sadness as she finished reading. "Oh, no," she said in dismay. "Poor Olivia and poor Jacob. They never got to see each other again."

"And poor little Jacob grew up with no daddy," added Christianne.

"Would Jacob Jr. still be alive?" asked Nick. "If he was two in 1920, that means he would be. . . uh, 94 now. Wow, that's really old."

"You never know," Mandy replied. "People do live to be that old. It would mean a lot to him to find out what happened to his father. I guess it also means the treasure is rightfully his." She looked at the envelope the letter came from. "Here's a return address: *Olivia Snow, 82 Burke Street, Baltimore, Maryland.* We should write to him."

"He probably doesn't still live there after all these years, if he is alive," Nick said. "Maybe, though, someone knows about him. Put everything in the box and we'll take it with us."

As they stepped into the hall, they heard a strange sound. A tapping noise seemed to be coming from downstairs.
The children stood still, staring at each other. Mandy held a finger to her lips to keep her cousins from speaking. Then she tiptoed down the hall to the top of the stairs with Nick and Christianne close behind her. They peeked over the broken railing, but it was too dark to see anything. The tapping continued.

"That's Morse code!" Nick whispered in astonishment. "Dots and dashes spell out words."

"Can you make out what it's saying?" Mandy whispered back.

Nick listened to the same pattern repeated over and over. "D – E – S – K, desk?" he said, puzzled.

Mandy snapped on her penlight and aimed it down at the reception desk. No one was there. The tapping stopped. "Come on!" she said, heading down the stairs.

"Careful!" warned Nick. "Don't rush. Remember the railing?"

After they made it safely down the steps, the children stood in front of the desk, waving the lights around. The tapping sounded again, this time with a different pattern.

Nick blinked and listened hard for a few minutes. "M – A – I – L," he said, "Mail."

"Is someone sending us a letter?" Christianne asked, holding tight to Mandy's t-shirt.

"The pigeonholes!" Mandy exclaimed. "That's where letters would go when guests got mail!" She rushed behind the desk and played her light over the openings. "Look! Number 26 – that's Jacob Snow's box – there's a letter!"

"That wasn't there before," said Christianne, shaking her head. "We would have noticed it."

"Someone – or some*thing* – put it there," whispered Mandy, "while we were upstairs." She grabbed it and rushed outside.

In the bright sunlight, the children shielded their eyes from the glare.

"Let's see what it says!" Nick said, reaching for the letter.

Mandy hid it behind her back. "Let's do it at the house. We need to open it carefully so we don't rip it."

As they headed to the house, they noticed the Sheriff's car parked outside.

"Uh, oh," said Nick. "Either Sheriff Bentley is here for some of Mom's chicken alfredo or something's up."

As they stepped into the kitchen, his mother looked up from the dishes she was drying. 'Oh, Nick," she said, "your dad wants you to come to the mine. He said to just head down the main tunnel and they'll meet you. They've found something he wants to ask you about."

Nick gulped. "Uh, what is it?"

"I don't know," his mother replied. "But they called in the Sheriff. The cave in looks suspicious, your dad said."

Chapter 22. The Mystery Deepens

With treasure and the letter forgotten for the moment, the children followed the tunnel in the mine to where they heard men's voices. Much of the rockslide had been cleared away and Mr. Vance, Sheriff Bentley and Nick's father stood talking near the skeleton of the Old Miner.

"Uh, hi, Dad," Nick said. "You wanted me?"

"We wanted to ask if you kids were playing around in here last night," his father said in a stern voice. "We've noticed things out of place since the tour yesterday. The fence here to the Old Miner is unlocked, there's a candle holder on the wall, and we found some chalk marks. Do you know anything about this? Be honest."

Nick shoved his hands in his pockets. "Well. . . um. . . yeah, we were here, but we weren't playing. We were looking for something. And we didn't put the candle holder there – someone else did."

"What?" his father growled. "You were in here alone after what I said just two days ago?"

"Yeah," said Nick, squirming, "but I can explain. Uh, uh, we wanted to look at the Old Miner up close because --" He glanced at Mandy and sent her a silent request for help.

Mandy jumped in. "We were looking at the Old Miner to try to find out who he is. I heard a 'thud' and the rocks started tumbling and the tunnel filled up with dust. We climbed up to a tunnel in the next level and from there, finally managed to get out. We think someone blew up the mine on purpose, sir."

Uncle Ross groaned. "Why on earth didn't you tell me, Nick? Never mind," he continued, "I know, you were afraid of getting into trouble. Which you are, but we'll talk about that later."

"There do seem to be indications of a blast instead of a natural cave in," Mr. Vance said. "There are some fresh drilling marks. Also, in the tunnel above we found a piece of new rope tied to an old ore cart with one end cut off. Do you know anything about that?"

"Cut?" asked Nick, his eyes wide. "Someone *cut* the rope?"

"We had a rope," explained Mandy. "That's how we were able to get out. But we thought the rope broke."

"Cut with a knife," Mr. Vance said grimly. "Obviously, there was someone here besides you kids last night."

"We should check the top of the cliff," Mandy said. "We saw a bright light up there last night after we got out of the mine."

"Do you mean the UFO?" Christianne asked.

Nick rolled his eyes and looked at Mandy, as if to say 'why did she have to mention that?'

"Let's all go," said the Sheriff. "I've been hearing things lately about lights in the middle of the night and unusual activity in the old mines. It's worth investigating."

They trekked out of the mine in single file.

"Show us where, Nick," the Sheriff said.

Nick led them up the hillside to the spot where the UFO had landed. . . or what they had *thought* was a UFO.

"Hmm, tire tracks," murmured Sheriff Bentley.

"Do UFOs have tires?" Christianne asked.

The Sheriff chuckled. "No, but ATVs do. That's what caused these marks."

"There are a lot of those around," said Mr. Vance. "They use the trails all over the canyon."

Mandy was thinking hard. "That would explain the lights. But don't ATVs have two headlights like cars? This was one bright light with some smaller colored flashing ones."

"There are a couple of those in the canyon," said Uncle Ross. "They've got some pretty big tires on them, too, which might match up to these treads."

"That's what the ATVs looked like that scared the horses on the trail ride yesterday!" Nick exclaimed. "Two guys wearing helmets rode straight at us!"

"Hmm," said Sheriff Bentley. "Let's look for footprints. We'll see if they got off the vehicles. Try not to mess up the site with your own footprints," he warned.

"And look out for snakes," Nick said to Mandy.

"I'm staying right here!" she declared. "Not moving a muscle."

Following the maze of tire tracks, the men studied the ground.

"Here!" shouted Nick. "Someone got off and on right here. Here's some round prints like the bottoms of buckets. They must have been carrying something." He followed the footprints over to a big rock. "That's strange. The footprints end here." He rested his foot on the rock, scanning the ground around it. "Whoa-o-o!" he yelled, scrambling and clutching for something to hold onto as he disappeared into the earth.

"Nick!" Mandy screamed. Her fear of snakes forgotten, she rushed over to where her cousin had been standing. "He fell through!" she called to the men. "There's a hole here!"

Chapter 23. Into the Earth

Uncle Ross aimed a flashlight down the hole. "Nick?" he called. "Can you hear me?" His voice sounded tight, like he was trying not to panic.

"Dad," Nick groaned, "help. . . something fell on top of me. I can't see anything."

"I'll be right down," said his father, crouching and ready to jump.

"Wait, Ross!" Mr. Vance produced a rope and tied it around Uncle Ross' waist. He and the Sheriff held onto it and lowered him into the hole.

Mandy and Christianne crowded close to the edge, turning on their penlights. They didn't shine far enough to be of much help.

Uncle Ross reached the bottom and snapped on his own light, which was more powerful. "Where are you, Nick?" he asked, swinging the light in a desperate circle.

"Here," said Nick's muffled voice, "underneath something. . . please hurry, it's hard to breathe." He wiggled his body, which made a pile of dirt and rocks move.

Nick's father scooped away the debris and lifted a sheet of plywood off his son. He shined the light on Nick's rumpled and dirty figure.

Nick took a deep breath and then choked on dust. "I'm okay, Dad," Nick wheezed. "Just banged up a little."

His father gathered him up in his arms and hugged him. "Thank goodness," he muttered. "I don't know what I'd do if something happened to you." He helped

Nick up. He found his inhaler on the ground and handed it to him. "Well, Nick, it looks like you've found another entrance into the mine. That explains how the trespassers were able to get in and out with the gates locked."

He scanned the walls of the tunnel with his light.

"Nick's okay! Come on down!" Uncle Ross called up to the rest of the group. "There's a ladder. I'll hold the light on it so you can see."

After their descent, everyone stood in the cramped space, looking around.

"Are you really okay, Nick?" Mandy asked her cousin, taking in his scrapes and dirt-streaked face.

"I'll live. Just watch that first step," he replied, giving her a weak smile.

"You don't look okay," his sister said. "You look like something the cat dragged in, like Mom says."

"Whatever," said Nick.

The men followed the tunnel, which slanted downward, and the children trailed behind. Everyone except Christianne had to stoop because the roof was so low.

Mr. Vance called, "We've got a shaft here with some steep rungs." He began climbing down, while Uncle Ross held the light.

At the bottom of the shaft, they shined the lights around.

Uncle Ross whistled. "This looks familiar! This is the tunnel above where the cave in happened." He led the way down the tunnel to the hole made by the blast. . Stooping down, he pointed. Right there is the miner's skeleton."

"The sounds we heard last night!" exclaimed Mandy. "The creaking must have been the bad guys climbing up the emergency exit ladder. From there, they took their own way out of the mine."

Uncle Ross held onto the edge of the hole and dropped down to the level below. He helped the others down.

The Old Miner still lay behind the fence, covered now with a heavy layer of white dust. The eye sockets, blacker than ever, stared at them.

Mandy thought he looked sad. Now that she knew so much about him and his life, she felt sad, too. His tragic death had affected so many people – his friend Queho, his wife and son, who waited and waited to hear from him and never did. She wondered what the letter said that they hadn't opened yet. . . and who led them to it.

"You know," said Nick, "we should check the candleholder for fingerprints. Whoever put it there are the same ones who drilled the hole and set the charge." His eyes widened. "And the ones who cut the rope I was hanging from. . ."

"Good idea," said Sheriff Bentley. "Here's the key to the cruiser, Nick. Would you run out and get the fingerprint kit out of the trunk? If you're up to it. If not, I can send your cousin."

"No, I'll do it," Nick said. He accepted the car keys from the sheriff and jogged down the tunnel.

"That's a smart boy you've got there," he said to Uncle Ross after Nick had hurried away, "and brave, too."

Uncle Ross hesitated and then smiled. "Thanks – yes, he is, isn't he?"

Sheriff Bentley frowned, deep in thought. "You realize don't you, that even if we identify the fingerprints, this is all circumstantial evidence? The most we can get these people for is trespassing. We need some hard evidence that proves they are the ones who set the charge and cut Nick's rope."

"What on earth do you think they are up to, anyway?" asked Mr. Vance. "Why would someone want to blow up the mine?"

"Nick thinks they tried to sabotage the mine so it would be unsafe and you couldn't have tours anymore," said Mandy. "You would have to close the mine. Then they would be free to drill in here all they want."

Uncle Ross played his flashlight over the uneven wall above the candleholder. The light revealed a series of holes. "They must have been exploring this quartz vein, using a chisel and hammer so they wouldn't make too much noise."

"With the price of gold as high as it is right now," said Sheriff Bentley, "they could make themselves a tidy sum if they had a way to get the gold out of the ore. They would need a lot of it, of course."

Nick returned with the fingerprint kit, breathing hard from his run through the tunnel.

The children watched with great interest as the sheriff opened the box. "Girls, shine your lights on the candleholder," he said, taking a plastic vial from the case. He sprinkled black powder on the rim of the metal holder and then whisked most of it away with a small brush.

"This is so cool!" said Nick. "I've never seen anyone dust for fingerprints before, except on tv."

"That looks like a good one there," Sheriff Bentley said, pointing at a dark smudge. He pressed a piece of sticky plastic against it, which lifted the fingerprint. He then stuck that to a white card. "There are three kinds of fingerprint shapes," he explained, "an arch, a loop, and a whorl. But every person's prints are a little different. I'll compare this one to the millions of prints on the computer database and hope for a match."

"Wow," Nick said. "I want to be an investigator!"

"I'd say you're off to a good start," the sheriff replied, winking at him. "Now, as I said, we just need to find some hard evidence. That's not so easy."

"What kind of things would be 'hard evidence'?" Mandy asked.

"Well, fingerprints on something from the blast or the knife that cut the rope would be helpful."

"Oh. . . right," she finally said. "That sounds impossible."

"Just about," Sheriff Bentley said, closing the fingerprint kit with a snap. "I'll let you know what I find out." He spoke with Mr. Vance and Uncle Ross for a few minutes and then headed out of the mine.

"I've been thinking," Mandy said, a frown on her face. "Is it common to have rock avalanches in Nevada?"

"Well," Nick replied, "mostly in the mountains, not so much around here." His face paled. "Are you thinking that someone might have caused the one at the spring on purpose?"

"I think we should go find out," she said. "Right now."

Chapter 24. The Ghost Letter

The three children trudged up a steep hill, with Nick on the lookout for snakes.

"We should. . . have. . . ridden," he said, gulping in air.

Mandy remembered her wild ride on the runaway Circus. "No," she panted. "This is. . . good exercise. You said this is a shortcut."

"It is," he said, halting at the top. "This is where the rocks fell from."

They peered over the edge down at the spring where the trail riders had stopped for a snack and been bombarded.

"So how would a person start a rock slide?" Mandy asked, looking around.

"They could push some rocks," Christianne volunteered, "or blow up the cliff! That's what the Wile E. Coyote tries to do to Roadrunner on cartoons."

Nick rolled his eyes. "He *never* gets the Roadrunner. You're right though, these guys seem to like blowing things up."

"Would they use dynamite?" Mandy asked.

Nick shrugged. "I heard Dad say that dynamite was used for blasting in the mines in the old days, but not now. There are other kinds of explosives though. I have no idea what they look like."

"Well, let's just look around and see if we find anything," Mandy suggested.

"What about this?" Christianne asked, prodding a metal tube with the toe of her shoe.

"Don't touch it!" Nick shouted, pulling her away from it. He set her to the side, and crouched down to get a closer look at the tube. The metal cylinder, about four inches long, had one open end and lots of dents. "I don't know *what* it is," he said, "but it has a smell like fuel. We should take it with us. But if we try to pick it up, we'll mess up any fingerprints."

Mandy pulled a ziploc bag out of her pocket. "Evidence bag," she said. "Just push the tube into it with a stick."

"Yay, Mandy!" Christianne cheered, giving her cousin a high five.

Back at the house, Nick handed the metal tube to his father and explained where they found it.

"I'm on my way to Boulder City," his father said. "I'll stop in and give the tube to Sheriff Bentley. It could have contained explosives so I'll ask him to test it for fingerprints. If someone did cause that avalanche, we need to find out. Who knows what they'll try next? Meanwhile, would you kids run down to the corral and feed the horses? I'll be back in a couple of hours."

"Did you tell your dad about the treasure?" Mandy asked, as they walked down the road to the corral.

"Not yet," Nick replied. "He was in a hurry."

"I'd like to read the letter first anyway," Mandy said. "Before we have to hand everything over. Obviously, *someone* wanted us to find it. So how do you happen to know Morse code?"

Nick grinned. "Some of us guys use it to talk with each other in class when things get boring. We use hand signals for dots and dashes. Pretty cool, huh?" He handed her a letter opener.

Mandy slid the letter out of the envelope, taking care not to rip it. "This is to Jacob Snow from his wife, too," she said, checking the signature at the bottom. "It's very short."

Dearest Jacob,

I have wonderful news! The man who killed the shop owner has confessed. All charges against you have been dropped! You are a free man. Please come home to us right away.

Your loving wife,
Olivia

"Oh, no!" said Mandy. "Jacob died before he got this letter!"

"That's so sad," said Christianne. "He didn't know it was okay to go home."

"He must have been accused of a crime he didn't commit – just like Queho," said Nick. "That must be why they became friends. Jacob knew what it felt like."

Mandy put the letter back in the envelope and added it to the tin box. "It must have been his ghost that did the tapping. He wanted to know what was in the letter. There wasn't anybody else around."

"Maybe it was," Nick said, sliding the box under his bed. "Stranger things have happened. I guess we'll never know for sure. Come on," he said, "we need to go feed the horses."

"Hi, Circus," Mandy said, giving the appaloosa a pat on the neck. She held out an apple on the palm of her hand and the horse snuffled it up. As she watched

Circus crunching it, she thought about explosions. "Nick," she said, "if the bad guys caused the avalanche at the spring with something in a tube and it worked, wouldn't they do the same thing to blow up the tunnel in the mine?"

Nick glanced up from the hay bale he was kicking around. "Uh, yeah, that makes sense. It would mean though. . ."

"There's another tube. . . in the mine!" Mandy finished for him. "We've got to find it!"

"Wait," he said, "don't be crazy. That would be like trying to find a needle in a haystack!"

"Just bring a magnet!" his sister said.

"Right," scoffed Nick. "The mine is *full* of metal."

"But we do know generally where the explosion happened," said Mandy, thinking hard. "In the tunnel above the Old Miner."

"The Sheriff and Mr. Vance already checked there," said Nick. "They would have found anything the size of a tube."

"Maybe, maybe not," Mandy said. "They didn't know what they were looking for. We have to go back."

Nick groaned. "Just when things are going well with Dad. I'll be back in the doghouse again."

"We don't have a doghouse," said Christianne, bewildered. "We don't even have a dog."

"It means he'll be mad at me again," her brother barked at her. "But if it means solving this mystery, I'll have to take the chance." He thought for a moment. "Dad took the tube to Sheriff Bentley in Boulder City. He said it's possible that an explosive had been packed into it. He won't be back for another hour. Come on, let's do it now. First though, I'm going to get a decent flashlight. . . and a new rope."

Chapter 25. The Search for Evidence

Ten minutes later, they headed into the mine. When they reached the Old Miner, they stopped to look at him.

"Poor Old Miner," murmured Mandy. "Jacob, we know you were innocent. Your wife sent a letter to tell you, but you never got to read it."

"Do you really think he can hear you?" Nick asked.

"Yes," Mandy replied. "At least I hope so."

"All right," Nick said, suddenly all business, "we don't have much time before Dad gets back. Start looking. If the tube was down here, I think Dad and Mr. Vance would have found it when they were clearing the tunnel." He flashed his light up at the hole in the ceiling. "Somehow we have to get up there."

"How about a human pyramid?" suggested Christianne. "Like the cheerleaders do."

"Good idea!" Mandy said. "You'll have to be on top – the flier."

Nick groaned. "Yeah, I can guess who's on the bottom."

"Well, you are the biggest *and* the strongest," his sister said, batting her eyelashes at him.

"Whatever," he muttered, handing her the rope and getting down on his hands and knees.

Mandy stepped on top of him. "Come on, Christianne, I'll give you a boost."

The little girl stepped on her brother's back. Nick groaned. Mandy made a stirrup with her hands and, bracing herself against the wall, lifted her up to the hole. Christianne gripped the edge and scrambled into the tunnel above.

"Okay," she said, "throw the rope up to me."

Mandy hopped off and Nick got to his feet, moaning and stretching his back. "Man, you girls need to go on a diet," he joked.

"You need to lift some weights," Mandy retorted and grabbed the coil of rope from the ground. She tossed it up to Christianne. "Tie it to the ore cart. Be sure to make *lots* of knots, tight ones."

When the end of the rope slithered down, Mandy caught it and hung from it to see if it would hold her weight. "Give me a boost, Nick," she told her cousin.

"I see who's last again," he muttered, putting his hands together for her to step into.

She grinned down at him and then disappeared into the hole above. Then her head popped into the opening. "Come on, Nick, hurry up."

He sighed and started climbing up the rope. As he struggled to get himself over the top, the girls grabbed his jeans and pulled. He plopped onto the tunnel floor like a large, flopping fish, gasping for air.

The girls left him there and started searching. Their flashlight beams showed only the rough floor and walls, and small piles of rock and rubble. They moved down the tunnel, all the way to the shaft where they had descended by rope the night before. Nick caught up with them.

"Nothing," Mandy said to him in a discouraged voice. 'We found nothing."

"Listen," Christianne whispered. "I hear something."

They stood still and listened. A snuffling sound seemed to be coming from back down the tunnel where they had been.

"It's the ghost dog," breathed Christianne. "He wants us to follow him again."

"Ghost dog," muttered Nick. "It's probably just a big rat."

"She was right last time," Mandy said in a low voice. "*Something* led us out of the tunnel last night. We could still be wandering around in the mountain looking for an exit."

The three children crept back up the tunnel. The snuffling turned to panting. They were almost back to the ore cart.

"Turn your lights off for a minute," whispered Mandy.

"Why?" asked Nick.

"Just do it," she replied, snapping off her penlight.

Her cousins did the same. In the total darkness, a faint glow seemed to come from inside the ore cart. Beside it stood the ghostly image of a large and lean white dog with ears pricked forward and mouth twisted into a snarl. It growled at them.

"Uh, oh," said Nick, ready to run.

"Wait!" said Mandy, grasping his arm.

With a single yip, the ghost dog faded away.

"He's gone!" said Mandy, turning her light back on. He wanted us to see him."

"I can't believe it – we just saw a ghost!" Nick said, shivering.

"I told you the ghost dog was real!" said Christianne. "He didn't look very friendly though."

"Come on!" said Mandy. She clambered over the last few yards of rough ground to the ore cart, with her cousins right behind her.

Peering inside, they saw the gleam of metal on top of the rocks in the cart. A metal tube, similar to the one they had found above the spring, lay beside a jackknife. The fancy knife had a stag horn handle adorned by the silver silhouette of a coyote.

"Wow," said Mandy. "The ghost dog wanted us to find these things – our hard evidence!"

"I've seen that knife before," Nick whispered. "I know who it belongs to."

Chapter 26. A Big Surprise

"We got the results of the fingerprints on the metal tubes and the knife," said Sheriff Bentley a week later. He paused and looked at the circle of faces around him. "They didn't match any in the database system, but thanks to a tip from Nick, we did find the culprits."

"Who was it?" asked Mr. Vance, his fists clenched.

"Why don't we let Nick tell us," said the Sheriff. "Tell us everything, Nick."

"Uh," Nick said, trying to get his thoughts together, "Well, when we found the tube above the spring, we realized the rockslide had been caused on purpose. Dad said an explosive could have been packed in it."

"That's right," his father explained. "ANFO, a commonly used explosive, is a mixture of ammonium nitrate and diesel fuel put into a tube. It's more stable than dynamite or nitro glycerin and doesn't cost much."

"So," Nick continued, "we thought there might be a tube in the mine, too, since we figured the same people blew up the tunnel. Sheriff Bentley said we needed to have 'hard evidence' so that's what we looked for."

"The ghost dog led us to it!" exclaimed Christianne, unable to keep quiet.

The adults smiled.

Mandy could tell they didn't believe her. "It's true," she said in a serious voice. "The ghost of the Old Miner's dog led us to the mine cart where the tube and knife were just sitting there."

"We did find fibers on the blade of the knife," put in Sheriff Bentley. "They're being tested, but I have no doubt they are from the rope that was cut in the tunnel which caused Nick to fall."

"Right," agreed Nick. "And I recognized the knife. One day a couple of months ago, a man who lives up the canyon stopped into the café for lunch. He was cleaning his fingernails with the blade and I said what a cool knife it was. So he showed me all the different blades and the silver coyote on its side. His initials are carved into the handle – J. M. for John Madder."

"That gave us enough to order a search warrant," said the Sheriff. "When we searched the Madders' place, we found more evidence. The shed out back of their house is where they keep their ATVs. Sure enough, it's those souped up models with the one big headlight surrounded by smaller flashing colored lights."

"Oh," said Christianne, disappointed, "the lights we thought were the UFO. So it wasn't ET."

Everyone laughed.

"Not this time," her father said. "But don't give up hope. People in Nevada do see a lot of strange things in the sky."

The Sheriff cleared his throat and continued. "We also found more of those metal tubes and the chemicals to make the explosive. Also, buckets of ore were sitting around. It seems that John and his brother Rick have constructed their own smelter, which separates the gold and silver from the quartz. Of course, it takes tons of ore to get enough gold to make it worthwhile."

"So they wanted the mine to close down so they would be free to go in and take what they want?" Uncle Ross asked.

"I think it was even more than that," Mr. Vance said slowly. "When the mine was up for sale ten years ago, they wanted to buy it. Before they could scrape up enough money, I stepped in and purchased it, recognizing what a marvelous chance it was to open it to tourists. Needless to say, they don't like me much. My guess is this is also revenge. They wanted to ruin me."

"Well, they're behind bars now," the Sheriff said, "since we had enough 'hard evidence' to arrest them." He winked at Mandy.

"While all this was going on, the kids were busy on another front," said Uncle Ross. "They discovered the skeleton in the mine was a man named Jacob Snow. By good detective work, they tracked down his room in the boardinghouse, which they shouldn't have been in" – he paused to glare at the children – "and found a tin box under the floor."

"The treasure!" said Christianne, her eyes gleaming.

"The box contained some interesting things," continued her father, "some Morgan silver dollars minted at Carson City in 1893 and a bag of gold dust."

"Wow," Mr. Vance exclaimed. "That *is* a treasure. . . and it was found on my property? Those silver dollars alone must be worth a small fortune!"

"Yes, but hold on," said Uncle Ross, holding his hand up. "There were also some letters. We were able to track down Jacob Snow's son in Baltimore. He and his daughter still live at the house on Burke Street. I gave them a call. Jacob was thrilled to find out what happened to his father. He asked if we would send his belongings from the boardinghouse. And, of course, the 'treasure' is rightfully his."

Mandy swallowed a lump of disappointment and shared a look with Nick. She knew they had done the right thing by contacting Jacob, Jr., but it was hard to hand over the treasure. Of course, if it hadn't gone to him, it would have stayed with Mr. Vance. Somehow, it didn't seem fair since they were the ones who found it.

"What about the skeleton?" Nick asked.

"Mr. Snow would like the bones returned so the family can give him a proper burial in Baltimore," replied his father. "I guess we'll have to find another skeleton for the tourists to look at."

Mandy was glad Jacob Snow would finally rest in peace. She thought probably his dog would, too. Somehow, they had managed to speak from the past to take care of unfinished business. And they had helped solve a modern-day mystery.

Aunt Ariel held a letter in her hand. "This just came in the mail. It's addressed to Nick from Jacob Snow, Jr. in Baltimore!"

"Wow!" said both Mandy and Christianne, crowding close to him while he opened the envelope with a butter knife.

Nick scanned the letter, his eyes growing wide.

"Read it out loud!" his sister demanded.

He began to read:

Dear Nick, Mandy and Christianne,
I can never thank you enough for locating my father's remains and his possessions. It means the world to know he

was preparing for my mother and me to join him until his untimely death. This answers a difficult question I have lived with my entire life: Why did he abandon us?

I appreciate your parents sending my father's clothing and letters. When his remains arrive in Baltimore, we will bury him in the family plot. It is strange to think I will finally meet him after all these years!

Concerning the coins and gold dust, please take out of that the expense of shipping the above. I would like your Mr. Vance to have the letter about Queho for his museum and the gold dust to help maintain the mine for his tours. I have learned the Morgan dollars of that minting are quite valuable, worth about $800 a piece. I really have no need of the money, as I did well in life as a business owner. So I would like you children to have the silver dollars. Put them in a college fund or whatever your parents think is best. I can tell you are smart, thoughtful children and will make good choices.

Thank you again.

Sincerely yours,

Jacob Snow, Jr.

The children stared at each other in stunned silence.

"He's letting us keep the silver dollars?" Mandy asked in disbelief. "Twenty times $800 is how much? $1600?"

"Add a zero," Nick said in a hoarse voice. "$16,000."

Uncle Ross grinned. "Very generous of him. Frankly, I think you kids earned it. You're turning into quite the investigators. You put Jacob Snow's mind to rest *and* saved the mine. I'm proud of you all. Just try to stay out of dangerous places in the future, okay?" He clapped a hand on Nick's shoulder. "And Nick, I'm especially proud of you. Your quick thinking at the spring kept the Forsythes from getting hurt in the rockslide. You also put two-and-two together to figure out who the culprits were in the mine explosion. I hadn't noticed how you are growing up!"

"Thanks, Dad," Nick said with a wide smile.

Mandy felt her spirits soar. Uncle Ross was proud of Nick at last *and* the treasure was theirs!

"Yippee!" Christianne yelled, "We're rich!"

"What will we do with all that money?" Nick asked, still grinning.

"Well, I think the college fund is a good idea," said his mother. "But a vacation would be nice, too. I've always wanted to see St. Augustine, Florida. Do you think your parents would like to join us there, Mandy?"

Mandy's eyes were shining. "Yes, I think so. And you know what? Dad said St. Augustine is the most haunted city in the United States! They have a haunted lighthouse, haunted fort, haunted jail, haunted inn. . ."

Nick groaned. "Oh, no," he said, "here we go again!"

Author's Note

Before writing *The Ghost Miner's Key*, I traveled to Nevada to visit the Techatticup Mine, a ghost mine in Eldorado Canyon. What an eerie experience to walk through the dark silent tunnels where hundreds of men once labored with chisel and hammer and two candles a day. The Techatticup Mine produced millions of dollars in gold ore, as well as silver, copper and lead. The work was dirty and extremely dangerous. A skeleton I saw in the mine, a chisel through its forehead, inspired the story of the fictional Jacob Snow.

The mining camps truly were a lawless place and killings happened all the time. The Indian outlaw Queho really lived in the canyon. A plaque at the mine credits him with the killing of 23 people, including the innocent Maude Douglas. However, some historians today question whether he really was such a cold-hearted killer or if he was blamed by law officers for many of the crimes in the area that went unsolved.

Also true is the legend of the Hell Dogs of Eldorado. Supposedly, when the town was abandoned, many of the miner's dogs were left behind, still chained in the mine. Now, some people say, their fierce ghosts haunt the canyon.

Morse code is a way of sending a message as a series of on-off sounds, light flashes or clicks that can be understood by a skilled listener or observer. The code uses short and long signals called "dots" and "dashes",[1] or "dits" and "dahs. Each letter or number is represented by a sequence of dots and dashes. The duration of a dash is three times the duration of a dot. Each dot or dash is followed by a short silence, equal to the dot duration. The letters of a word are separated by a space equal to three dots (one dash), and two words are separated by a space equal to seven dots. The most well-known message sent in Morse code is SOS, the signal for distress, which is three dots, three dashes, three dots. *from Wikipedia

International Morse Code

1. The length of a dot is one unit.
2. A dash is three units.
3. The space between parts of the same letter is one unit.
4. The space between letters is three units.
5. The space between words is seven units.

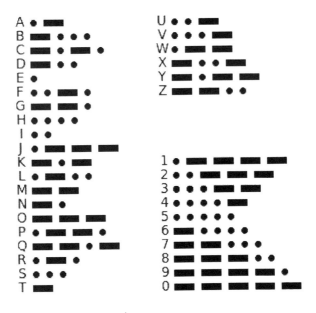

Learn how to dust for fingerprints and solve crimes at a great website for kids:

www.cyberbee.com/whodunnit/dusting. html

Try your hand at solving fun combination lock puzzles, a free math game, at another website for kids:

www.combinationlock.com

BOOKS BY ANGELI PERROW

The Key Series for 8-12 year olds:

The Lightkeeper's Key
The Whispering Key
The Ghost Miner's Key

The Celtic Series for teens:

Celtic Thunder
Celtic Tide

Picture Books:

Captain's Castaway
Lighthouse Dog to the Rescue
Sirius the Dog Star
Many Hands: A Penobscot Indian Story
Dogsled Dreamer

To learn more, visit:
www.angeliperrow.com